WARMTH

LUCAS AMANN

Copyright © 2022 Lucas Amann.

All Rights Reserved.

Cover Art by Lucas Amann.

Layout and Formatting by Christian Francis.

The characters and events in this book are fictitious. Any similarity to real persons, living, dead or undead is coincidental and not intended by the author.

No part of this book may be reproduced in any form or by any electronic or mechanical means, including information storage and retrieval systems, without permission in writing from the publisher, except by a reviewer who may quote brief passages in a review.

Encyclopocalypse Publications
www.encyclopocalypse.com

For Dad

And for Mom and Leanne,
my brightest lights

CONTENTS

ONE

A ROMANTIC NOTION

Orange strobes swell, rupture, spill waves of cooling violet into infinity, a plasma garden flourishing from and retiring to the inky loam of outer space. Ethan drifts, boundless as the flames. It's not so far away as the stars seem. He only has to close his eyes.

His mom calls from downstairs, for the third time now, and suddenly he's back in his bedroom, submersed in the cool blue glow of the teal Christmas lights he hung earlier while his dad was out doing the roof. "Coming," he yells, no intention to follow through. His aunt, uncle and cousins are down there. It's nothing against them, but

he doesn't get why they care if he joins anyway. They're clearly having fun without him, to judge by the laughter. And he already said hi, so.

He squints his eyes and watches a phosphene burn itself out, leaving dim echoes to blossom anew, only fainter, ever fainter...

It's barely an hour since the sun itself expired, and the void's already sucking at the warmth it left behind, nibbling at Ethan's nose and ears. He cranks the dial on the space heater set up by his bed. It whirs and glows brighter. Unusually cold night for mid-December, at least by Sugar Land standards. Been that way all week. He sparks his Bic, traces the flame around his rainbow-striped socks. There's this neat trick he learned a while back, but you have to catch the lint just right. When you do... *whoosh!* A flash of dancing amber takes off flowing across his foot like tiny wildfire, consuming all the stray fibers.

Laughter interrupts Ethan's reverie. Not the affected merriment booming from below, but a more distinct snicker, nearer. His youngest cousin, he thinks at first, spying on him from his door? No. The window, fogged with sweat-streaked condensation. A ghostly visage presses the glass. "Eth-uhn," it lisps, sounding to anyone else unrecognizable. But no lisp, no dose of helium, not even a crowd of a thousand competing voices could disguise this one. Not from Ethan.

He bounces out of bed, draws his hand into his sweater sleeve, and mops the frosty pane. "I'm 'thuck," Fox says, tongue writhing like a helpless slug, pinned by his flattened face. Ethan thumps the glass, and Fox jumps, yelps, breath visible. Someone cackles. Wait, is Pete with him? Ethan thrusts the window open to find them huddled together on the eave, which overhangs the fence for an effortless climb.

"Getcho dancin' shoes, boy," Fox says, in his best Texas twang, "we gon' get rowdy tonight." He's got on the women's windbreaker straight out of the eighties he found at a Goodwill store a while back. Neon geometry, shoulder pads, the whole works. That jacket means trouble, Ethan knows too well. Fox only wears it when he plans to go off.

"Hope you thirsty." Pete tightens his bandana headband, unzips Fox's backpack and makes a withdrawal: Mad Dog 20/20, blue raspberry. Must have gotten lucky badgering people outside the corner store. He takes a swig, and his features implode into the bridge of his nose. "Tasty."

Ethan can feel a grin breaking across his chapped face. It's not so often Pete hangs with them anymore, and that really hurts Fox, Ethan can tell, even if Fox would never say so. Seeing them together's an incredible relief. It means Ethan doesn't have to feel so guilty about what he's been thinking. It means Fox maybe won't be alone after all.

"I can't," Ethan says.

"Why not?" Fox stuffs his hands down the waistband of his school-issue gym shorts, warms them there. He's not bashful about that sort of thing. Nor, apparently, about wearing those outside of P.E. It's one of the things Ethan really loves about him.

"My cousins are here."

"Not like you're even hanging out with them," Pete says. "You're just fuckin' with your lighter."

"Yeah." Fox tips himself forward and spills head-first through the window, feet banging the glass as they flip through after him.

"Shhh," Ethan hisses, worried someone downstairs might hear.

Fox hunts down a pair of scattered checkerboard slip-ons, tries to wrestle Ethan's technicolor feet into them. "Get ya little shoesies on, let's go."

"Stop." Ethan giggles (he can't help it) and kicks free. "I *can't*."

Fox looks up at him, eyes crossed. He balloons his cheeks, bursts them with the soles of Ethan's shoes. "Life is now, Ethan. Blink and you'll miss it."

"Yeah, you keep saying."

"S'what Miss Woolley tells us," Fox says, shoulders

shrugged, as if that should lend credence to its wisdom. He springs onto the bed, strokes fur angels into the shaggy turquoise comforter.

"So you're saying you actually learned something?" Pete drops in with a good deal more grace.

Fox flips him off.

Pete flips the light, momentarily blinding everyone.

Ethan's room used to be really carefully designed, with lava lamps and drip stick candles, this cool old fiber optic light that looks like a firework paused mid-burst, and all this other retro shit he was really into for a while. His parents helped him fix it up a few years back when they redid it from the kiddy room it used to be. They even found these really neat aluminum shelves to display all his snow globes (he has almost fifty now, including one with a shrunken head Fox made for Ethan's fifteenth birthday last year). But he's really let the place go since then, basically the way old people do their bodies.

Fox snags a marker from the nightstand, pops the cap, clamps his tongue between his teeth, and goes to work on the mural he's been continually building upon since this girl, Felicia, left a kiss-print that Fox couldn't resist recontextualizing with a doofy face. Now almost the entire wall behind Ethan's bed is covered in Fox's art. It's Ethan's favorite thing about his room.

Pete throws up his hand. "Great, we're drawing now?"

Fox flashes his lopsided grin. The one that shows off his dimple and the small gap in his teeth. The one that makes Ethan fucking crazy, especially with Fox's cheeks flushed the way they are from the cold. It's weird, when you really love someone, it's their imperfections. And Fox is nothing but.

"When did Ellie get home?" Ellie is Ethan's older sister.

Fox just heard her laughing downstairs. She's really putting on a show down there. Ethan wonders if she's actually having fun or if she's just that good at pretending.

"Last week."

"What? No way. Tell her to come to the creek." He's had a thing for Ellie since she drove them to a bunch of haunted houses last year. She was a senior then, but she's in college now, and Ethan misses her so much.

"Come on, man." Pete takes another swig. "Lez go."

"What you need me for?"

"Yeah, hey, good question." Fox caps the marker, tosses it onto desk, slouches so that Ethan can see he's been drawing a skull. "What we need him for?"

"We just do."

"Oh yeah, that's what I was thinking. Yeah, we just do."

You don't, though. Not really.

"Ethan!" That's Dad this time, and his heavy footsteps are plodding up the stairs.

Ethan can't stop glancing at Fox. It's the way the Christmas lights twinkle in his watery eyes. They're aimed at the end of the street, headed for the tree line. The air's got that stinging feel that somehow makes things more alive. Fox keeps asking about Ellie. How long's she here for? She still dating that douche from that lame band, what was it called? Think she might want to get high or something before she goes back?

"Dude," Pete finally blurts, puffing a breath-cloud into the cool.

"What?"

"You're obsessed."

"Nah, I'm not. I'm obsessed with this one." Fox captures Ethan in a headlock, presses his lips to Ethan's ear, and shoots it with humid breath as he whispers, "I'm totally obsessed with you, E."

A charge flutters through Ethan, electrifying the fine hairs on his neck, and the slightly coarser ones on his forearms, making the boundary between him and the world scream hot and cold at once. *Christ*, he thinks, blushing like a spanked ass, *he doesn't know what that does to me*, and makes a show of shoving Fox away.

They skid down the graffitied concrete slope of the culvert to the steaming creek below. Fox digs the blueberry yuck back out from his bag, drowns his gullet, then, fighting to keep it down, offers the bottle to Ethan. Ethan's got this thing about drinking after other people, even family, so he usually wipes the lip on his sleeve, but it's different with Fox, so he skips that step and kisses the bottle's lip, just a taste test to start. *Eek.* Like a popsicle blended with rubbing alcohol. Whatever. He takes a big enough gulp to satisfy his friends.

Pete hikes the legs of his jeans up over his knees and carries his shoes to the stream. Is he really gonna... ? Yep, he takes a few tentative steps into the water. Where his feet land, dirt billows, clouding the otherwise transparent flow.

"Cold?"

"Nah, kinda warm."

Fox's eyes pop. "Serious?"

"Come on."

Fox stabilizes himself on Ethan's shoulder, brings his legs up one at a time and pries off his skull-print Vans. He hands 'em to Ethan and turns his back. "Couldja help me out please, feller?"

Ethan stuffs the shoes into Fox's backpack, zips it up.

"Thanks, boy." Fox snatches the bottle and skips out into the water, leaping and howling like a cat dumped into a bath. "Shit-fuck that's cold, you liar!" He sloshes to Pete, pounces onto his back. Pete hoists him and wades downstream with the hundred-some-pound load.

Ethan crosses a fallen tree to the opposite bank and follows along, haunted by the image of his family as he saw them through the windows on his way out, 'round the side of the house. Like a scene from a holiday commercial, all sweaters, smiles and steaming mugs. How fitting that he should be on the outside looking in. He's felt that way as far back as he can remember, not just with his family, but in life generally.

He paces himself behind Fox and Pete, swinging on the occasional tree so he doesn't get ahead. He likes to watch the two together. Been friends so long, they might as well be brothers. His own history with them doesn't run as deep, even though the back of his neighborhood butts up to theirs. Some invisible dividing line routed Ethan through different elementary and middle schools. Entering freshman year, he was so terrified he wouldn't make any friends, that he'd find himself lunching alone as he had through much of eighth grade, but he met Pete in AP Biology first period that first day, bonded over Pete's Tool T-Shirt (the one with the dick wrench), and come lunchtime, as Ethan resigned himself to a solitary spot at the end of a relatively vacant table, Pete spotted him, called him over, and introduced him to Fox, who, as it later turned out, shared his gym period. Reflecting, they seem so young. They may only be sophomores yet, but they've been through shit together. The kinda shit that carves your life into eras, splits who you are from who you were. This year, Pete lunches with his lacrosse team. Fine with Ethan, not that he doesn't love Pete too, but he shares most of his classes with Pete, and sometimes lunch is the only time other than the bus that he gets to see Fox at school at all. They've gotten so much closer, Ethan and Fox, reduced to a pair. True, the pseudobrothers share a bond Ethan couldn't begin to compete with, but there's this whole other thing with Fox, this whole other side to him Pete doesn't even know exists. Like Fox has this color, invisible to a colorblind world, only Ethan is allowed to behold. It shines for him, and him alone.

Ethan's phone vibrates. He pulls it from his pocket. *Dad.* He rejects the call.

"Sippy-sip?" Fox holds the bottle to Pete's mouth. "There you go, yeah, suck it down you naughty twit."

A cloud of blue mist explodes out of Pete along with a fit of choking laughter. "Dude." That one even wins a grin from Ethan. Fox's clowning has a way of grounding him when he's lost and tangled up in his own head.

"Yah! Yah!" Fox bounces, beats his foot against Pete's thigh, spurring him onward.

"Hey, so... my dad said we can start looking at trucks," Pete says.

"Yeah, boy!" Fox reaches 'round, grabs himself a handful of Pete's chest, thrusts his pelvis at Pete's back.

"Fucking stop." Pete pries Fox's fingers from his nipple and shrugs him off into the water.

"My knee," Fox howls. Hurt it once jumping off Pete's roof onto his trampoline. Never got it fixed, so he's always throwing it out.

"Don't twist my tit, then." Pete slogs on, no hint of concern or sympathy.

"Sorr-*ie*. Ethan loves it when I twist his tit."

"Shut up," Ethan says, laughing to mask his discomfort.

Fox hobbles to catch up, his haste throwing waves over the muddy banks of their usual hangout.

Ethan and Ellie used to come out here fishing for minnows when they were little; Pete and Fox, for BB gun wars. Pete still has a tiny ball lodged in his belly from when Fox pumped his rifle ten times and blasted him from all of maybe fifteen feet away, as Pete tells it. You can roll the BB under the skin, push it around with your finger. Ethan can attest; he's felt it. Lucky they both still have their eyes. Besides that, Fox used to hide his weed here in little graves he'd mark with sun-bleached soda cans, back before Ethan knew him, back when his mom still cleaned his room. So, there's history here, but, really, the boys didn't start coming out together until toward the end of last year—that's when, well... Fox's dad died. A heart attack, just out of nowhere. It totally destroyed Fox, *destroyed* him. He's mostly better now, but there was a while Ethan thought Fox might never laugh or joke again. He'd never seen anyone hurt like that. That's when they, by then a trio, made this their refuge. A place where they could go and not be found, a place where the rest of the world could just fucking fade for all they cared.

This spot in particular's cool 'cause there's some tile and shit from an old house that must have burned down or something. And what used to be a hot tub, bit further back, filled with toxic green sludge, breeding ground for mosquitoes, cottonmouths, and God knows what else.

The boys settle into the exposed roots of the trees. Pete doesn't think anyone's looking, so he grips his bicep and flexes, checking its girth and tautness. Bad habit he picked up when he started working out last year. Ethan checks Fox, but Fox isn't seeing; otherwise, he'd burn him, no doubt.

Fox hands Ethan the bottle. Ethan takes another swig, wipes the blue from his lips, face knotted in disgust. "Might as well bought Draino."

"I like it," Fox says, laughing.

"You would." Ethan passes the bottle.

"I do."

Pete battles down a swallow. "Why can't we sneak your dad's shit anymore?"

"My mom's gonna freak if she finds out."

"Thought she didn't drink."

Fox snatches the bottle. "What happens when she looks in the cabinet, dumbass?"

"Oh, I'm the dumbass?" Pete pulls out his vape pen. It's an act of aggression. He knows Fox hates it. It's the one vice Fox'll turn his nose up at.

"Cool," Fox says.

"Don't judge me, asshole." Pete's cloud drifts directly to Ethan. Never fails. Boy's a magnet for smoke.

"What's that, s'mores?" It's always something strange like that, and always different.

"Toasted marshmallow," Pete says, and offers the vape.

"Sure," Ethan says, cool as ice, as if he doesn't always refuse weed, cigarettes, *anything* that comes his way except alcohol, and often even it. "Why not?"

Fox flashes his eyes: *great.*

Ethan doesn't know what he was hoping to feel—not this —but Pete's already forked over the vape, so really, why not?

"Dude, what is up with your hair lately?" Pete says, smirking.

Fox rakes his fingers through his chaotic cowlicked mess. "What?"

"You need to comb that shit."

No, he doesn't, Ethan thinks. It suits him perfectly.

"Nah, dude. My do's fire. Ladies all a'tizzy, kid you not."

"What ladies?"

"Summer, for one."

She's this girl Pete's been pining over since, oh, basically forever? So that's Fox's way of getting back at him. Really, Summer likes Pete too, everyone knows it, but it's just this thing that never seems to happen.

"Shut up."

"No, I'm serious. We were in art the other day and she was all like, 'oh Fox, your hair is SO cute,' all, like, touching it and shit and saying, like, 'tell Pete his hair is boring,' and I was like, 'nah, man, *rude*, Pete's my friend,' but she was like 'no, but he needs to know,' so I was like, 'yeah, okay, good point, maybe you're right.' So, yeah. That's pretty much how it went down. Sorry, man."

"Uh-huh."

"But I don't know. Maybe if you, like, bleach it, or frost the tips, or, like—" his eyes burst wide like they do when sudden inspiration takes him, always by surprise. He scoots close to Pete, starts running his fingers through the meticulously styled locks, pulling them this way and that. "Yeah, I know *exactly* what to do. Yeah-yeah, we'll get you all fixed up. Shave all this, comb this over here, pull all this that way, and get some gel in here."

"Okay." Pete swats Fox's hands. "You can stop touching me now."

Ethan's only half here. That's his usual M.O., but right now, he's on edge because his dad's calling again. Freaking out, no doubt, since Ethan left the house without telling.

"What you think, Ethan?"

Ethan rejects the call, looks up. Fox has arranged atop Pete's head a coif with more twists and turns than a hedge maze. Ethan grins despite himself. "You know what, it actually captures something about you."

Fox appraises his work, hand at chin, nodding with the self-satisfaction of a sophisticate evaluating a museum piece. "Totally."

"This sort of delicate complexity."

"Exactly!"

"I'd definitely have Fox style you 'fore you finally ask Summer out."

"Stop picking on me," Pete says, good humored, and shakes out Fox's handiwork.

"Wait, wait! You didn't let me get a picture."

Pete grabs the bottle and takes a swig. "But really, you think I should ask her out?"

"Definitely," Ethan says. "Why not?" That seems to be his motto tonight.

"Oh yeah, hey, guess who was asking 'bout you at practice today."

Great. This again. Been there a million and one times already. "I told you, I don't like him."

"Yeah, but why not, though?"

"Who, Jay?" Fox asks, trying to keep up. Jay's on Pete's lacrosse team. Pete sometimes brings him around.

"Just because he's gay doesn't mean I have to be interested."

"Yeah, just because he's gay doesn't mean Ethan has to be interested."

"I just think you should give him a chance, man. He's pretty cool."

Fox scoffs. "For a meathead."

"Just because he plays lacrosse doesn't make him a meathead."

"No, being in the bottom ten percent of our class does."

"Aren't you in the bottom ten percent?"

Fox snorts. He's a good sport, but he goes all distant and spacey for a bit, as he does when he's hurt. Ethan aches for him. Fox isn't dumb. He's just, uh, excitable, which makes him difficult to educate, as more than a few of his teachers have complained. It sucks that people sometimes write him off for that, because he's sensitive too, which it seems like Pete sometimes doesn't realize, or else care.

Without his cheer to liven things, they're left in awkward silence, listening to the gurgling stream and watching Pete try to blow smoke rings. Ethan wishes he could move closer to Fox. Wishes he could tell him how special he is, even if it sometimes seems no one else realizes it. Wishes he could tell him that he came into Ethan's life like a light into darkness, and all Ethan's worst thoughts scattered like cockroaches.

Times like these, when his light dims, they come out again.

Do it right here, after they go. Might as well.

Ethan snags the Mad Dog, still nearly a third full, and turns it up—make that empty. He fights like hell to keep it down. It's touch and go for a second. When he looks up, Fox and Pete are eyeballing him like he's some body snatcher. He hurls the bottle. It smashes against a tree and explodes into a hail of shards that pelt the stream.

"Dude," Pete says, super annoyed. He's always picking up after everyone, discarding litter in random garbage bins on the walk home. It's just the kinda guy he is.

Fox goes off giggling as Ethan falls back. "What was that?"

Staring up through the canopy at the starry sky above, Ethan can't help wondering about Fox. If he's happy. Ethan really hopes so. He knows Fox still sometimes cries at night. Fox told him that much. But Ethan hopes he's happy otherwise. He gets an itch to ask, but he really kinda doubts anyone would admit if they weren't. He asked his dad once. *Of course*, came the reply, without hesitation, without thought. *Yeah, me too*, Ethan said. But if Fox said he was and really meant it, it might be easier to tell. Fox is easier to read that way.

Ethan props himself on elbow to study him.

Fuck it, I'm just gonna ask. "Are you happy?"

Fox's face ripples. Ethan caught him off guard. "What?" He snorts. "Like right now?"

"Just always."

"Yeah."

It took him a second, but Ethan thinks it's the truth. Or maybe not. Who knows? It makes Ethan so sick to think it's because of the worst thing to ever happen in Fox's life that they're as close as they are.

"You happy, Pete?" Fox asks, which makes Ethan think it must be a legitimate question.

"Yeah, man," Pete says, and unloads his lungs. "I'm good. You, Ethan?"

"Yeah." Ethan flashes a smile. Fake, but no one seems to notice. The thing he can't figure out is if anyone's really happy the way he means, like, as a general state of being, and not just a serotonin high from hanging out with friends, or whatever. It's not like he's sad all the time, but he just can't remember ever feeling happy except for a spattering of moments.

Pete gets up and makes for the trees.

"Need help?" Fox jokes.

"Yeah, wanna hold it for me?"

"You betcha," Fox says, chipper as a kid in some juice commercial. He blasts his cupped hands with two squirts of warm breath and rises to follow.

"Fuck off." Pete shoves Fox, and disappears shaking his head. Few seconds later, you can hear he's more than capable, his stream splashing into the toilet that once was a hot tub.

Ethan: a sailor, lost in a storm of thoughts.

Fox: a lighthouse tower; his scrutiny, a thousand kilowatts.

Ethan meets his gaze, and Fox smiles down on him. Not that dimple-accompanied side-grin Ethan finds so dizzying. No, he's concerned. Silently asking if Ethan's okay.

Yes, Ethan tries to answer with his own smile, another lie. But this one's more obviously forced.

Fox throws himself down...

Sweeps his arm so the backs of their hands just barely touch. Ethan's pulse races as he turns his hand palm-up and parts his fingers, allowing Fox's to invade and entwine. *Why are you doing this?* Ethan silently begs. It's not the first time they've held hands, but it's the first time Fox has initiated, and it's definitely the first time they've done so where someone else might see.

Ethan's been out since fifth grade. His dad even took him to Pride that year. Mom worried about nudity and "inappropriate behavior," but Dad took him anyway. Their secret. So, yeah, Ethan's totally cool with it and has been all along, but for some reason, it's harder for Fox. And Ethan's tried, but he never wants to talk about it either.

Fox uses his thumb to caress Ethan, to pet the web connecting thumb to forefinger. *Weird,* Ethan thinks, *why's he doing that? Trying to reassure me, or...*

"What's wrong?" Voice so quiet, a dog would need a hearing aid.

Nothing, Ethan mouths.

Pete returns and Fox yanks his arm back. "Everything come out okay?"

"Saw a snake."

"No, you didn't," Fox says, wanting to believe.

"Looked like an anaconda."

Oh. "Sure it wasn't a skink?"

Pete flips him off.

"Shit!" Fox suddenly springs to his feet. "What time is it?"

Ethan sits up and checks his watch. Two 'til ten, Fox's school-night curfew. No way he makes it in time. "Better run."

Fox digs into his backpack, crams his mouth full of mints, douses himself in cologne, slings his bag over his shoulder. "Okay, bye-bye. Don't have too much fun without me." Fox takes off weaving through the trees.

Turn around, Ethan silently begs, hoping for a final snapshot to hold onto, *just turn and smile.*

He doesn't.

So, if I do this, that's it. That's the last time I see him. Ethan hugs his folded knees, plants his face into the scratchy denim.

"S'it just me, or is this chem final gonna be a massacre?"

Ethan laughs. "Total bloodbath."

"Watch, you prob'ly ace it."

"No way."

Pete climbs to his feet, brushes himself off. "Let's go get warm, man, you want?"

"Think I might hang out. I just don't wanna go home yet, ya know?"

"Oh." Shifting eyes, scrunched brow. Ethan just hopes he won't think too much about it. "Okay..." Pete says, uncertain. "You cool?"

"Definitely, yeah. You go ahead. I'll see ya tomorrow."

"Alright, man, later." He lingers a second... then off he goes.

A cold wind sends dry leaves twirling, skittering across the muddy shore, down into the creek. Ethan follows to the water's edge, dips his fingers, shudders. Eyelids clenched, he replays Fox's backside, cutting through the trees, but rewrites history so he gets one last dizzying smile cast over Fox's shoulder.

Ethan picks up a crunchy oak leaf, sparks his Bic, and sets it ablaze, twirls the torch by its stem... then drops it atop the icy flow. The flame sputters, clings to life, then dies in a gasp of smoke, leaving red-orange embers to glitter in the night, drifting into utter darkness downstream. Powerful, the feel of early autumn the fragrance of burning brush conjures. But Autumn's almost gone, and Spring's not coming for a long time yet.

Ethan pries off his sneakers, tosses them over his shoulder, then swallows a raspy breath and sinks both feet into the frigid water, into the sludge, making stormy dirt clouds billow.

Not so bad, he thinks.

Then, possessed by a sudden impulse, he scoots forward, drags ass into the bath-deep flow, and draws a sharp intake of breath as the water meets his balls, saturates his jeans and the tail of his sweater. He reclines, elbows planted in the sediment, lolls his head so he can stare up into the speckled void, where one star—no, a plane—scrapes the others. He wishes upon it anyway—

I wish... I wish for Fox to find a way to be as happy as he used to be.

He eases himself all the way back, until the gush washes his face. *Would it be possible*, he wonders, *to do it this way?*

He blows all the air out of his lungs...

But his body betrays him, launches him upright, gasping for breath.

He peels off his soaked sweater, tosses it ashore, watches the water drip from the strands of hair dangling at his eyes, his humid breath clouding the cool air before him. He clamps his jaw to stop his teeth chattering.

There's a reason babies come screaming into this world, he realized once; the very state of living, of *being* is such a profound discomfort. Over time, you're supposed to grow accustomed to it, or busy yourself enough to distract from it. But he hasn't, can't.

He dredges the silt for a piece of the bottle he smashed. His fingers find something sharp. He brings it up. A transparent shard. Moonlight waltzes all along its shiny wet edges. Pretty.

I wonder if Fox is home yet. I wonder if he'll think of me.

Fox enters through the garage. It's quieter. At least if the door doesn't squeak. It does.

"Fox?"

He winces, freezes. That's Mom. Sounds tired too. Did he wake her? "Huh?"

"Did you just get home?" Her voice nears. That means she wants to talk. "It's a school night."

"It's the last week before finals," he says, routing himself though the kitchen to evade her. "All we're doing's watching movies and sh—stuff." The Oreos are out, so he crams one into his mouth and makes off with a stack of five or six more. "Night," he shouts from the foot of the stairs, spraying crumbs all over, "love you!" He races up to his bedroom before she has a chance to interrogate him. He doesn't know why he even has a curfew. No one else does.

A motion-activated Halloween skull goes off cackling as he enters, plastic eyeballs rolling wildly in their sockets. Place is full of skulls and skeletons, but that one's his favorite. He loves its stupid eyes. So, yeah, this is Fox's bedroom. First time Ethan came over, he joked that it looked like an ossuary or something. But the bones have nothing to do with death or, you know, Dad or anything. His mom asked him that once, which he thought was really weird, 'cause he had most of that stuff up before. He just thinks they look cool.

It's cold as balls in his room, so he kicks off his shoes and leaps into bed, goes all the way under the covers. Inside the fabric womb, he lights up his iPhone, untangles his earbuds, and navigates to YouTube. He's been listening to this band, Psychic Brine, he discovered fully by accident last week. They've only got two songs, muffled DIY recordings, less than a hundred views between them of which Fox accounts for roughly half. Nothing special if we're being honest, but for whatever reason they move him. It's insane to Fox that no one's taken notice. He left a comment on one of their videos the other night. He didn't know what to say, so he just put a fire emoji. Just wanted 'em to know that someone appreciates them. *It's gotta suck*, he was thinking, *putting your soul into something, and, like, everyone just shrugs.* He tried playing one of their songs for Pete, but Pete wasn't impressed. Ethan said he liked them, but you never know with him. He'll go along, not to damper your enthusiasm.

The videos are just black screens. Watching them's like staring into a rectangular abyss. Sometimes you can see something moving in the darkness. Probably just an optical illusion or compression artifacts or whatever, but Fox wonders if the band might have hid something in there. You bet, that's what he would have done.

He turns over onto his belly, Psychic Brine battering his eardrums. He starts to get a little hard 'cause he's thinking, next time it's only the two of them, he's pretty sure he might try and kiss Ethan.

Pete's got a queasy feeling it might have been a huge mistake, the text he sent Summer: *Ethan thinks I should ask you out.* Five minutes, and still she hasn't responded. *Ugh.*

He lies back. Vaulted ceilings. Skylight above the bed. Amazing when it rains. Big too, Pete's room. A museum of cool shit. His dad travels a lot, so there's stuff from Japan and Malaysia and Argentina and wherever all else. Bunch of drawings and photographs by friends, professionally framed. Some works given to him, others purchased at school art sales. At just fifteen (verge of sixteen), he's a full-on patron of the arts. His favorite piece: a plaster mask that Fox made in Sculpture 1. One of a series of three, his cast from Fox's own face, lots of little devil horns. Ethan possesses the companion cast of Pete's horned face, which means Fox owns Ethan's. Fox had the idea they might wear them this past Halloween, but they turned out really brittle, and the other boys, more precious about them than he was, decided they'd rather keep them as art.

Pete melts off the edge of the mattress, into a heap on his floor, takes up his guitar (Les Paul, lotsa stickers), but his hands are too trembly to play.

His phone buzzes on the bed beside him. His pulse pounds in his ear as he picks it up.

Summer's response: *I think so too.*

Ethan presses the point to his left forearm.

Do it.

Come this far a few times before, never further. There was this kid, Noah, in middle school, blew his brains out in his bedroom while his parents were on a date or something... and his twin sister, Noelle, was downstairs. Gnarly. When Ethan thinks about it, he pictures Noelle sitting on the sofa, playing with her phone when—*BANG! The fuck was that?* She goes upstairs to get Noah 'cause she's thinking home invasion or burglars or something, and she's just terrified out of her mind. When she knocks, he doesn't answer, so she opens his door...

Ethan can't remember if that's how it was told to him or if he painted the details himself. Anyway, seed planted, probably. But there was also this other guy. What was Ethan, nine, ten at the time? When his dad's coworker hanged himself? Kinda pathetic. *Better to go young*, he decided, *while there's still something romantic about it.* He only wishes everyone could feel the way he feels, just briefly, so they would understand and not hold it against him, or themselves.

He fights off an image of his grieving family... Mom, Dad, Ellie... sobbing. That gets him crying too. But the truth is, he's thought about this every day since seventh grade. *Every. Single. Day.* That's, what? Three, four years he's given them. He tried, but he can't do it anymore. He just can't.

What about Fox?

Doesn't need him. Has Pete.

Don't be a pussy. Just do it.

Yeah, *okay.* Here we go... blood gurgles and spurts, surprisingly warm, like liquid fire cascading over his left forearm. He draws the shard from his wrist to his elbow fold, scraping bone, and his arm parts down the center, opens like a pop-up storybook—*Inside Out* by Ethan Enders, Ages Fifteen and Up.

Pain? Yes, considerable pain, but that's not important now. Never will be again. Rest is coming.

His blood clouds the water, flows downstream in puffy swirling ribbons.

Glass scalpel in hand, he crawls, woozy, back up the muddy beach.

Cut the other one.

But his left arm's too mangled. Fingers don't work. Can't grasp the blade. Fading fast now anyway. Going dim. Just as long as no one finds him, he'll be okay.

Red rivulets race down the sloped terrain to the stream,

diverted along ridges, pooling in shoeprints... trickling into a rabbit hole.

Another cold breeze sweeps through, and a flurry of leaves part company with their branches, come twirling down. Ethan looks up, tears streaming...

Please just be over. No heaven, nothing. Just please be over. Goodbye. The End.

TWO
COLD FLESH

Fox jolts awake, a vague impression of his mom's voice resonating in his recent memory. Dream or reality?

"Fox?" That's her, knocking at his door, voice carrying a hint of... concern?

"I'm up, I'm getting up," he says, and kicks off the covers, wipes the crust from his eyes. *Weird, why's it so dark still?*

His mom enters, triggers the battery-powered skulls. "Have you seen Ethan?"

"Uh, no? What are you talking about?" *Wait. Why's she wearing pajamas? She's always dressed when she wakes me. And —phone muted against her thigh—who the hell's she talking to, anyway?*

"He didn't come home last night."

"What?" Fox rips out of bed.

"Do you know where he might be?"

He yanks on a dirty T-shirt (inside out), checks the night table for his phone—absent. Back onto the bed, he pistons his arm between mattress and headboard, paws around until he finds it, usual hiding place (damned thing). His thumbs shoot all over the screen, stabbing out messages: *hey / where you at / you okay??*

His heart pounds ferociously in his chest, such a frantic, irregular rhythm that it almost feels like there's a squirrel, gerbil, *something* trapped and turning itself all around, desperately seeking escape. Please, *please*, he silently mouths.

No response comes. No ellipses, nothing. Just radio silence.

You need to come home, his mom said that night. Worst phone call of his life. He knew then, somehow. From those words alone. Whether by her tone or by psychic intuition, he just knew. The same way he knows now—

No.

He wedges his bare feet into his loosely-tied skull-print sneakers, rockets off, phone in hand.

"Where you going?" But he's already gone.

He launches through the front door into a liminal world caught between night and day. Subtle violet glow. Patches of frosted dew yet to thaw. Far too cool for the gym shorts and T-shirt he's wearing, not that he gives a goddamn. He strides across the crunchy grass, jams his phone to his ear.

Pete barely manages to pry one bleary eye open, and answer. "What?"

"Is Ethan with you?"

"No?" Pete sniffles, crunches over his knees, wipes the wet rims of his nostrils on the sleeve of his thermal undershirt.

"Did y'all go somewhere after I left, or... ?"

"No. We split right after. Why?"

"He didn't come home last night."

"Shit. What?"

"Do you think—"

Something about the hesitancy in Fox's voice scares Pete. "What?"

"I'm gonna check the creek."

Pete peels himself from bed, steps into a pair of jeans, tries phoning Ethan himself, to no avail.

Fox's long strides become a brisk jog, become a full-on sprint...

He reaches the tree line, skids down the concrete slope of the culvert, momentum hurtling him into the water with an explosive splash, and a pop of his knee. Back to his feet, he slogs downstream... stopping a few yards out, slowing in horror when he sees—

"Ethan?" A choked whisper caught, mangled somewhere in his throat. "*Ethan,*" he tries again, a little louder, too scared to approach. He notices the red-stained earth... the opened forearm, practically hollowed out. Space aplenty for a family of small songbirds to nest down in. "Oh fuck, oh god," Fox's trembling hands meet his face.

He starts walking, wading through the ankle-deep water, kicking up mud clouds, sending minnows and water striders racing.

An agitated crow shrieks—*stay back, stay away*—then takes flight.

Water sloshes in, foams out of Fox's sneakers as he steps ashore and approaches... squish... squish...

"Ethan?" His voice is barely a rasp. He kneels beside something once so pure and good, beautiful. Now just... a body... a *thing*. Perfectly still, alien. Lips bluish, mouth slightly ajar. Eyes open slits, irises milky.

Fox takes Ethan's hand and shudders...

"Oh fuck, Fox. He's dead. Is he dead?" That's Pete, standing right behind him. He just sort of teleported here, as far as Fox can tell.

Fox turns over his shoulder, face mangled to hell. "He's cold."

"Oh shit. Oh fuck. Did you call nine-one-one?"

All this time, Fox realizes, he's just been, what? Sleepwalking? *Wake up. Do something. Where's your fucking phone? Oh, there it is, in the mud. Must have set it down or dropped it or something.*

"Yeah, hello, it's my friend..." Pete's already on it. "I think... I think he tried to kill himself or something. Oh my god... His wrist. He cut his wrist, like, all the way up his arm... he's fifteen... no, he's not conscious. Is he breathing?"

Fox keeps drifting, sailing, where?

. . . That night, that call from his mom, her voice the stuff of nightmares, and he already out of his mind on shrooms—*you need to come home*—the firetrucks outside, all the people inside, some terrible party he arrived late to, and... just a glimpse before his mom intercepted, took him to the very edge of the lawn, where they sat crying, the wet of the grass seeping through the seat of his jeans, shrooms sucking, clawing him into their vortex of despair... he clinging to Mom, clinging to sanity... until there was no one left but them...

"*Fox*, is he breathing?"

Fox snaps present, drops his ear to Ethan's mouth, listens, feels for breath. "No."

"No, he's not, he's not breathing. Is there a pulse?"

Fox jabs his fingers into Ethan's neck. "I don't know, I don't think, I can't feel anything."

"No. There's no pulse... no, not really. I mean, it looks all *coagulated*, like..."

"Come back, please, come back..." Fox whispers, stroking Ethan's hair.

"I don't have an address. We're at the creek by Ravenhurst. It's the end of Lakeforest drive... Pete Harris... No, my other friend is here. Do you know CPR? *Fox!*"

CPR? *Yeah, er, kinda.* Learned it in Health. *Come on, E, come on, come back.* He tilts the head, wipes some spittle away, pinches the nose, performing the steps as he recalls them...

Never so much as a kiss between them, and now he hesitates... seals their mouths together.

"Yeah, okay. Hold on, hold on." Pete fumbles to put the phone on speaker. "Can you hear me?"

"Yes, I hear you." That's the operator's voice, calm and reassuring, amplified by the device's tinny speaker. "I have first responders on the way. One of you needs to start CPR and the other needs to meet them at the road, show them how to get there, okay? Can you do that? Is one of you able to perform CPR?"

Fox peels his lips from Ethan, looks up, horrified. He doesn't want to split up.

Pete doesn't either, judging by the torture he inflicts upon his shirt neck. "Yeah, okay. Okay. I'll go." He sets his phone on the ground beside Fox. "I'll take yours just in case," he says and snags it, thrusts it at Fox to unlock.

"I don't know how to do this," Fox pleads, thumbing his passcode. *Click.*

"I'm gonna talk you through it, sweetie, okay?" says the operator.

"Okay."

Pete checks Fox once more. Neither is okay with this. He takes off anyway, splashing down the creek. It's all up to Fox now.

"Where's your friend?"

"He's on the ground."

"Can you lay him flat?"

"He is."

"Okay, good. Place one hand on his forehead, the other under his neck, and tilt his head back."

"Okay..."

"Open up the airway. Put your ear next to his mouth and confirm if you hear or feel any breath."

Fox tries, but the jaw's tight. *Oh fuck, oh God, what does that mean?* "I can't, I can't get his mouth open, oh, God."

"That's okay. We're going to start compressions."

"Okay."

"Take the heel of your hand and put it on the center of his chest, right between the nipples."

"Okay."

"Place the other hand on top. We're going to press hard and fast thirty times, okay? Two inches deep."

"Okay, okay."

"I want you to count out loud with me, as fast as I'm counting..."

He begins pumping, stops immediately because—

Ethan wheezes! *He's alive!*

"He made a noise! He's making noises! Ethan!"

"Is he conscious?"

"I don't know. He's not waking up! Ethan?"

"We need to keep going, keep counting, honey, come on..."

Fox joins her, counting out each compression. The operator goads him faster, faster, *faster still*. An impossible pace. "Come on, Ethan. Please, *please*."

Those sounds, those wheezes, it begins to dawn on Fox, are just a byproduct of his own manipulation, just air he's pushing through, like a musician performing on this most gruesome bagpipe. Strange, how you can hear the character of Ethan's voice in the raspy exhalations. "Are they coming?"

"They're coming, honey. They're on the way. I know it's hard but we have to keep going until they take over."

His voice trembles. "I think he's dead."

There's a short pause. "Keep going with the compressions, okay?"

The thought of wailing on a corpse—*Ethan's corpse*—is just too much for Fox. He turns full control of his body over to the operator, who performs on Ethan through him with her counts.

A million years pass, then—

Sirens. In the distance.

"I hear them. They're coming."

"Don't stop until they take over."

Fox wipes sweat from his brow, resumes pumping...

Finally, *finally*, help arrives.

Fox looks over his shoulder, expecting the paramedics to rush in and relieve him. Instead, they slow. He keeps pumping, as the operator instructed. But why, *why* don't they hurry?

An eternity, then one of the men kneels beside Fox, places a hand on his shoulder. Fox falls back into the mud, scrambles out of the way, brings his trembling hands to his face. The EMT doesn't pick up where Fox left off but simply lingers over Ethan.

He's dead. I knew it, he's fucking dead.

Fox gets up and paces out into the creek, hands on the back of his head. He shuffles twenty, thirty feet from the scene and collapses onto hands and knees in the water, vision dim, bursting with phantom sparks, hearing filtered as though through a seashell. A muffled voice reaches him from a million miles away, one of the men telling Pete there was nothing the boys could have done, that Ethan's been gone a while.

Orange explodes. Violet swells. Fire blooms in darkness.

Fox watches phosphenes dance on the twin screens of his tightly shut lids, coming together to form a glowing Rorschach of Ethan's lifeless face. A ghostly after-image burned into his vision. It keeps fading, but Fox jams his knuckles into his eyes, presses harder, harder, willing him back, holding him there and renewing until only disconnected splotches persist... and themselves eventually fade.

No telling how much time has passed, but when Fox finally opens his eyes again, policemen are present. One of them's questioning Pete, whose cheeks are streaked with tears.

He's crying, Fox thinks, *why am I not crying?*

The sun pierces through the morning gloom, radiant and beautiful, casting rays down through the dead canopy to dapple Fox's bowed back, warm his trembling body. Looking down, he realizes for the first time that his shirt's inside out... and smeared with blood.

An iridescent beetle rafts by on a leaf, its lifeboat. Its faceted eyes bulging, panicked.

Hi Mr. Beetle.

Hiya, sport. Say, I seem to find myself in a spot of trouble. Be a pal and lend me a hand?

Oh, sure, no problem, here you go. Fox scoops the beetle, flings it ashore.

Thanks, kiddo!

Don't mention it.

"Ethan!" a banshee cry trumpets through the seashell-filter of Fox's ringing ears, spurring his every molecule to toll in sympathetic (dis)harmony. It's Ethan's mom, Gina, slipping, sliding, scrambling along the muddy banks—and, oops, there goes her foot, right into the water—trying to keep up with Ethan's dad, Graham, to get to her boy.

Fox turns, watches.

Upon arriving at the—hate to say it—*body,* Graham sort of... howls? That's the only word that really comes close to describing the horror that comes out of his mouth. His legs give, and he falls into the mud, sobbing. "Oh, no, no, no, no, no..."

Fox's eyes hunt and find Pete, nearer the action. Pete finds Fox too, and they share the misery of the moment together, then Pete looks up suddenly, past Fox.

Fox follows his gaze...

Ethan's sister, Ellie stands a ways off, hugging a tree, staring, horrified.

At what, me? No, Fox realizes, *this blood on my shirt. My god, all this blood.*

Police escort Fox and Pete from the creek, bring them up through the gathered emergency vehicles and looky-loos (joggers and retirees mostly, stopped for a dose of morning excitement) to meet their parents.

Fox watches as a school bus passes—*their* school bus— windows peopled with gawking pimpled faces, and, yep, there's their seat, second to last row, empty, but not for long because this mop-headed freshman, RJ Boyd, launches in from across the aisle, jams his face and palms against the glass, curious to see what all the commotion's about.

Fox watches with vacant wonder as the bus rolls on by.

How does the world go on?

THREE
AFTERIMAGE

Fox hugs his bare legs, enveloped in steam, shower striking him like a spray of pinpricks. The dial's where he usually sets it, but his body temperature's way down, and the hot-cold collision points sting like fire. The heels of his feet, pink and itchy, promise blisters, the result of tromping through water in loosely-tied shoes, no socks. His bad knee aches fiercely, didn't even realize until now, probably from his fumble off the culvert slope. Probably should have told his mom the first time he fucked it up, gone to the doctor, oh well. She's downstairs making oatmeal, *just in case* he feels like eating. Called in to work so she could be with him, but, honestly, he just wants to be left alone.

Is that... blood? he wonders, looking at the red-tinged dirt underneath his fingernails. Then, while checking out his paws, he notices the wrists, the veins. An entire network, teal and sprawling under the translucent leather wrapping. *What would it take?*

"Fox?" Mom calls from just outside the door.

"Yeah?" he answers with a voice that sounds, even to him, not his own.

"Just checking. You've been in there a while."

"Oh..."

"Do you want to come out and try eating?"

He's in bed now, wrapped up in an electric blanket his mom dug out of the linen closet. Strange musty smell, but it's something. Mild comfort. He's watching one of those Psychic Brine videos on his phone, which for the life of him he can't remember getting back. Last he remembers, Pete had it, yet here it is in his hands, little worse for wear, few patches of dried mud Fox picks at mindlessly while staring into the rectangular abyss.

He's pretty damn sure it's not just a blank screen, but footage of a *really* dark room or a hole or cave or someplace. All he knows is that's where he wants to go, into the void, where the only thing that exists is this amazing song no one but he cares anything about.

His reverie's interrupted by a group text from Summer to him and Pete: *Did something happen to Ethan??*

Fox pictures their faces, all the kids at school, slight grins (just can't help themselves) as they spread the news. Like Ethan's some hot piece of gossip and nothing more.

The message disappears, leaving Fox to his darkness. Moments pass before Pete's response pops up over the void—

He died.

Summer: *I'm calling.*

Suddenly, the music's too intense. Fox rips the buds from his ears, leaps to his feet and paces, hands in hair, unsure what to do. What *can* he do? He can't even fucking cry.

That's when he sees it mounted on the wall among the plastic skulls: the plaster mask he cast from Ethan's face, thorny with a dozen little devil horns. He thumbs its cheek, chin, lips.

Weird, here he is.

He takes the mask to the mirror on the back of his door, holds the pale visage to his own.

Pete told Summer everything. She had skipped third period to phone him (tried to call Fox too, afterwards, make sure he's okay, but he wouldn't answer). Pete cried his way through the story and Summer cried too just hearing it, just hearing the quiver in his voice, promised she'd come be with him, very first thing after school. So here he sits counting the minutes at his open window, blowing toasted-marshmallow-scented vapor-rings into the warming day, trying hard to picture anything, *anything* other than Ethan there in the mud, there in that blood.

"Pete?" his mom asks softly through the door in her heavy Argentinian accent (Pete's accent more closely resembles that of his Texas-born dad, but he is fluent in Spanish, and sometimes dips in and out of both languages while conversing with Mom).

"¿Qué?" he asks.

"I smell burning."

"It's a candle."

"Do you maybe want to get out? Go somewhere?"

He thinks a minute... "I'm cool."

Like Fox's mom, she's home for the day. She and his dad had debated a while, who would go off to work and who would stay. Life goes on. "Whatever, why don't you both go?" Pete had said, overhearing the conversation, to their mutual embarrassment.

Pete checks his watch. *Is it time for fucking school to end yet?*

Three days have passed. For Fox, years... or maybe only minutes. *Time's so fucked up.* And not a peep from Pete. Why does that feel deliberate? Fox almost broke down and texted him once, but what could he even say? *I miss him, Pete, I miss him so much*, was what he started to write. *Yeah, no shit.* He erased the message and crawled back into his mental hole.

His mom went out yesterday and bought him a new suit so he wouldn't have to wear the one from... well, you know. He's wearing it now as they enter the parlor (with well-worn sneakers: not the skull-print Vans he usually kicks around in, even though they've since been washed and dried—he feared they might be inappropriate—but an older pair with a sole that flaps at the heel). Everyone keeps calling it a service. He doesn't know if there's a technical difference between that and a funeral, or if it's just a nicer thing to say, but he doesn't appreciate the implication people are obliged to attend. Can't remember if that was the word they used at his dad's... *whatever*. He was pretty out of it then. Probably there's just no good name for something like this.

So... word got out, it seems, and there's several kids from

school that Fox only kind of recognizes. Kids from Ethan's A.P. classes? Or his old youth group? Who knows. Who cares. This is so not Ethan's thing anyway. All this churchy bullshit. All these, what are they, lilies? Carnations? Whatever all these boring white flowers are. Fox and his mom sent a bouquet too, of course, but Fox searched and *searched* for something as colorful and special as Ethan was. Must have been the twentieth, thirtieth site he visited before finally he found this twisty, spiky arrangement with screaming oranges and ultraviolet purples. The moment he saw it, he knew it was the one, knew it was Ethan, although... he doesn't see it anywhere in any of these parlor rooms, so probably the family must have found them tasteless or something. Should have just let his mom order the white and pink ones she had picked out.

She goes off to speak with some people she recognizes. Fox mills around looking at the framed photos. In most of the older pics, it's just Ethan and his dad. Maybe just pretending, but the kid looks genuinely happy. Special relationship they had. Maybe he *was* truly happy then. Maybe it was adolescence that wrecked him.

One of the pictures features the three boys—Ethan, Fox, Pete—Halloween last year, the night Ellie took them around to all the haunted houses, when their friendship was still sort of tentative and newish, where Ethan was concerned. Ethan's wearing a jack o'lantern shirt. Fox can feel the corners of his lips twitch, their best attempt at a smile. The result's outwardly imperceptible.

"Nice suit." Pete's just come in. He's not wearing one himself, just the charcoal button-up and black chinos he wore to homecoming.

So here they are, together for the first time since that

horrible day. "I'm..." Fox's voice breaks into an unintelligible rasp.

Pete steps forward and holds him. "It's okay. Everything's gonna be okay."

How could this be okay? How can everyone keep saying that? "I tried to help him," Fox barely manages to choke out.

"I know."

"I tried."

"I know that. It's not your fault."

But it is. Ethan needed him and he wasn't there. Ethan was always, *always* there for him after his dad and all that, but when Ethan needed him, where the fuck was he? How did he not know something was wrong? He did, though, didn't he? "What's wrong," he even asked. So why, *why* didn't he do something? And, *oh, God*, what he said that night in Ethan's room.

"I said we didn't need him."

"What?"

"That night. He said, 'what do you need me for,' and I said, 'good question.' Why did I say that?"

"You were just joking, he knew that."

"I need him."

"I know."

Everyone's being ushered into the service now, filing into the pews.

On his way in, Fox notices Ethan's Dad, Graham, sitting alone in the back by the double doors, hunched over, utterly broken, lost in a framed picture of his boy. Fox longs to reach out to him, but instead follows the train of people moving up the aisle and takes a seat next to his mom.

There's no coffin or anything. Like Fox's dad, Ethan's been cremated, so, like Dad, Ethan's only memories now.

Ellie guides Graham up to the front pew. A pastor steps up to the microphone, clears his throat. That's when Fox notices, right by the big photograph of Ethan are *his* flowers, in all their twisty, spiky, retina-searing glory. The family must have liked them after all, enough to put them front and center.

It's a mess. The pastor doesn't know or care about Ethan at all. He's so inept, it's a fucking joke, and not a funny one, either. Most of what's he saying's all about how bad it is to do what Ethan did. When he offers up the microphone to anyone who might want to add a few words, there's an awkward tittering silence. *Someone say something. Make these goddamn losers understand how special Ethan was. How wrong the world is without him. Someone just say something, anything at all,* Fox rages, humiliated on Ethan's behalf that no one seems to care enough about him to speak, to turn this charade into something personal, meaningful.

I should say something, he thinks, and dries his sweaty palms on his thighs. He tries to work up the courage to stand, heart kicking savagely in his chest, but finds himself paralyzed.

The pastor clears his throat, prepares to move on. Fox opens his mouth to say, *wait,* but nothing comes out.

Then Pete stands, heads to the mic. Fox could just give him the world's biggest hug.

"Hi," he says uneasily. "Ethan was... Ethan was always," he stammers, fiddling with his tie, "sort of like this mystery to me..." He stops, gathers his words. That doesn't matter. It doesn't even matter what he says. It's enough that he's up there, but what he says is so beautiful to Fox, it hurts.

After the service, Ethan's Mom, Gina, finds Fox and holds him for a really long time. Long enough that he starts to wonder if maybe she knows about him and Ethan. "Thank you for the beautiful flowers."

"You're welcome," he says, even though what he really wants to say is, *I'm sorry, so sorry I failed him. I didn't mean to let him go.*

It all ended an hour ago. Fox is out at the creek now, still in his suit, just staring at the spot where Ethan... where he... *yeah.* Fox couldn't figure out what to do with himself when he got home, so he just started walking, no destination in mind. This is where his legs brought him. You can't really see where all that blood was anymore. You'd never even know that one of the two worst things that ever happened on this earth, as far as Fox is concerned, happened right there.

Wonder if it all went into the ground, he thinks and grabs a stick, starts poking, half-expecting blood to ooze from the punctures, part of him sort of wanting to see—and part of him very much not—if that proves to be the case.

Blood? No. But *something* does gurgle out of the soggy muck. Some kind of clear nectar with tiny fluorescent orange beads suspended throughout, like... like this vanilla-mandarin Japanese soft drink they used to sometimes get from the corner store. The cloying fumes find Fox's face, far sweeter than he recalls. Downright caustic. He shuts his trap. To even breathe through his mouth might risk rotting his teeth. Undeterred, the scent finds ingress through his nostrils and charges, burning through his nasal cavities. Fox sneezes, and, as if by sympathetic reflex, the ground does too—

An opening erupts with a sound like a belch fed through Pete's wah-wah pedal, and geysers that viscous shit all over Fox's new suit. "Fucking Christ!" he shouts, fumbling onto his ass and scrambling out of its range. He watches as the fountain decays to a trickle, then he crawls back on hands and knees.

There's a gurgling tunnel now, diameter of a ping pong ball, no telling how deep, venting air, hot and humid as a lover's breath, inner-walls fuzzed with a web of orange filament. Not in tropical birds or venomous frogs—not in all the world—has nature produced a color that vibrant. Fox yelps and rears back as a wave of proliferation shoots out from the opening like a pulse of flame across an alcohol-soaked surface, drawing fibrous sprouts of turquoise from the sodden earth. A second concentric pulse, and a third, radiate to water's edge, and in the span of a single wheezing gasp, Fox finds himself bedded in a lush lawn of, *wait*, polyester? A bit like Ethan's faux fur comforter. No, *exactly* like it. Fox notes, two-o'clock of his right knee, a tuft of matted fur glued by a crust of petrified who-knows. Always wondered. Never asked. How many hours has he spent lying on Ethan's bed, picking at that very spot?

He reaches out to stroke the tuft... hesitates just shy of contact, sensing—is he insane?—sensing life, *soul*, a charge of anticipation, the very charge he felt in the moment before Ethan first held his hand, sizzling in his fingertips, and in his prickling arm hairs. And is it his imagination, or do the fibers themselves prickle, strain to meet his touch?

Then the tunnel flares once more and—*Bloop!*—expels a plastic capsule. Kind you get from a quarter machine. Only, working up the nerve to take the gift into hand, Fox finds that it doesn't contain a cheap prize, but rather a live cockroach, real savage fucker, hissing, hurling itself at the plastic walls, desperate, hoo-boy, *desperate* for freedom.

Fuck! Fox drops the capsule. It lands with a nasty wet clack of the roach's rattled body, and rolls, slowly at first against the dense polyester brush, then picking up speed across the balder slope of the beach, loathsome abomination tumbling, helpless. It hits a root and catches air, lands bobbing in the stream, then sets sail for the Gulf, or wherever the water terminates anyway.

Bon voyage, creep.

Bloop! Bloop! The productive hen-hole lays in rapid succession two identical capsules, each with its own six-legged prisoner. Tumble-tumble, splash. Send my regards to Galveston.

Fox thinks to run and get Pete, but before the message can even reach his feet—

"Peek-a-boo!" A man's enthusiastic, muffled voice calls out from below and roots him in place. *Christ, what the hell? Someone's down there,* burrowed underground, as impossible as that sounds. But then, how is any of this possible?

Panic coils 'round Fox's throat, and constricts. Fear, God, fear of the kind he thought he'd finally put behind him. What if, *what if*, he never left that trip? "Hello?" Gasping, strangled.

"Peek-a-boo," the playful voice repeats, and giggles.

"Who is that?" False bravado, slight tremble, Fox

flooding with adrenaline, visions of evil clowns and shit dancing in his head. He lowers his face, braves a peek through the earthen peephole.

Straining his rods and cones for all they're worth, he can barely make out, beyond webs of orange fiber ignited by traces of seeping sunlight, that the tunnel expands an arm's reach below to a grave-like hollow, dimly lit, not by stray sunbeams but from within, by the faintest pale green radiance... by... yuh-huh, by plastic stars. Like those plastered all over Ethan's ceiling.

Open aperture, long exposure: an image develops. A face, there in the shadows. "I see you," it says.

Fox's every last nerve ending fights to solo in a symphony of alarm. Hot, cold, clammy, sharp, burning, Christ, burning!

"Yes I do."

"Who the fuck is that!" Spittle spatters Fox's chin. The vein in his forehead rages, *lemme at 'em*. Protective? Who, Fox? This little patch of land? Only consecrated in death with Ethan's own precious blood. Protective, you bet. But that's intellectualizing it, and Fox is working on instinct. He just wants this intruder—whoever, however—gone.

He rips off his suit jacket, whips it aside, yanks up his sleeves, and plunges his hands into the earth. What poor shovels those ten blunt fingertips make. What pisspoor rakes, those brittle fingernails, so soon jammed with tiny shard-like pebbles. And oh, what a fight the ground gives, patches of blue fur, believing to be actual grass, clinging for dear, dear life to unbroken soil by a tangle of dayglo-orange roots or, *what*, mycelium. *The fuck is this shit anyway?* Spun, woven, it would seem, from the threads of a friendship bracelet, the very kind Ethan used to wear.

"Peek-a-boo!"

And that voice. Fox recognizes it too. "Mr. Enders?"

He springs to his feet. Quick, pacing survey of his surroundings. He finds among the trees, covered under a skirt of rotting leaves, a relic of the house that once stood, and burned: remains of a shattered and charred ceramic pot, deeply embedded in dirt. He pries up a curved triangular plate half as long as his forearm, leaving its imprint crawling with millipedes. Weighty. Sharp. Not half-bad for a makeshift spade. Back to the dig.

And what difference the proper tool makes. Fifteen minutes later, you'd think the beach had been mortar-shelled, and there Fox squats, a soldier in a, *uh*, foxhole. He draws back, depleted, aching most severely in his knuckles, and all down his spine. He wipes his sweaty brow with the heel of his mud-caked hand, painting a streak of blue across his forehead. No sign of any intruder, but what alien soil is this? The ordinary copper brown of the surface yields to a soft, wet marbled substratum, like a van Gogh night sky of violets and ultramarines, and speckled too with a constellation of buried stars. Five-pointed plastic paste-ons, but stars nonetheless.

A sudden ambient charge floats the hairs on Fox's neck. The scent of ozone promises rain, and soon, but the thunder that follows comes rumbling not from the horizon, but from underneath him. Dense clouds of icy vapor vent from hiccuping pockets of flatulent clay and surge up in a boil of billows to a height of some ten or twelve feet overhead, where they hang together like a great seaswell suspended mid-break, frosty particulate glittering through the spiralling crest as the wave topples, splashes down in a tumble of curls that break cold and tingling across Fox's upturned face, and across the shelled beach.

And from those same hiccuping pockets, fountains of that gooey vanilla-mandarin drink gush and dwindle, gush and dwindle, sending orange-beaded rivulets sidewinding down the scalloped walls of unearthly clay to lie in melting coils about Fox's feet. He shifts his weight, peels one sole from the sucking sludge; his shoe print wells with a burble of thin groundwater overtop which the slow-sluicing syrup piles.

Light glints. He throws his gaze—

Those stars, they crawl, inch along on undulating isosceles limbs, bouncing sunbeams off their glossy carapaces, undersides flocked by oscillating orange cilia, Fox now sees.

And no sooner does he than, everywhere at once, life erupts, pours from the clay like ants from a kicked mound.

First come the worms, thread-thin and wriggling. Or, no, not worms, but half a million apexes of that friendship mycelium that trace the contours of dug earth, twining like serpent lovers into twisted helixes, braided cords, an arterial tree, endlessly branching into a fleece of capillaries. And from those brambles spring the most astonishing blooms, show-offs each and every one. But what talent!

One bud, facing an apparent identity crisis as it condenses from the frayed tip of a knit stem, transmutes from pearl to rubber to chrome on its way to becoming something kin to a snake rattle, and from there—tight coils slackening, melding, translucent-yellow keratin clarifying to a scuffed plastic nucleus set in pedals of neon poly foam—a baby rattle. Its beads swirl faster, faster, until they blur, and then phosphoresce, coming to resemble an imprisoned ground-spinner (Ethan's very favorite of all fireworks, Fox recalls, dinky little ground-spinner, of all things). Spastic light show, soon blotted by scorch marks, snuffed by a heavy discharge of trapped smoke. The spinner fizzles—BANGS!—and the blackened vessel fractures, as if composed of solid obsidian, crumbles, leaving only its bottom hemisphere clinging to its stalk, stepped by conchoidal cleavage, orbited like a dead planet by belts of its own debris.

Elsewhere, a bud of plasma flares up from a spire of orange filaments fleshed by upward-flowing rivulets of rainbow wax leached from the alien soil as a drip stick candle reverse-melts itself into existence. The flame runs blue, then crystallizes and opacifies into a painted C9 Christmas light, just like the ones hung in Ethan's bedroom, last Fox saw. Yet again the bulb changes form—or, more accurately put, relinquishes any rigidity of form—as its bulk surges into its tip and the thrust of that migration reverberates throughout its elongating figure. It departs the wick, rises like a glob of molten paraffin in a lava lamp; all the skies, its mineral oil. Another flame ignites, and the process begins anew.

Everywhere, flowers like these: shapeshifters phasing through whatever material belongings they know to imitate, some looping infinitely, others dying on the vine. This much Fox accounts in seconds, paralyzed by astonishment.

And then, the skulls.

Each no larger than a raspberry drupelet, marching on tiny thread legs in lengthy trains along the vines. Not just any skulls, but miniature replicas of the very ones hanging on Fox's bedroom walls. And not a funeral procession, but a parade. The distinct impression of joy, celebration.

And, bless him, Fox grins, *actually grins*. What infectious lunacy is this, this mad carnival of possessions?

Beneath him, the clay shifts, decays like so much piled sugar washed by a wave. A dozen saucer-sized sinkholes cave to reveal deep burrows furred with tufts of blue, home to very curious ground dwellers that rise and descend, rise and descend, in a hypnotic polyrhythmic dance. Ethan's snow globes.

Among them—*no, couldn't be.*

Heart pounding in his chest, Fox reaches out to pet it, but it shrinks from his touch, retreats shyly into its hidey-hole.

It's the globe he bought himself from Goodwill, gutted and redesigned to showcase a shrunken-head Halloween prop, then refilled, repainted, and gave to Ethan for his fifteenth birthday. But how can that be here when Fox knows damn well it's on display in Ethan's bedroom?

"Peek-a-boo! I see you!"

Fox whirls, catching just a glimpse in his spin-smeared periphery as someone—is it indeed Mr. Enders?—bobs down into a man-sized hidey-hole, and disappears from view. The pooling groundwater flows around Fox's feet, chasing the figure down the shaft.

"Mr. Enders?" Fox calls, mystified how the old man could have beat him here from the service, and got into the ground anyway before Fox dug it all up.

A cool breeze whistles through the branches, scattering a flurry of autumn leaves across the beach, some twirling into the dig, and into the man's burrow. Fox adjusts his grip on his ceramic shard and steels himself for battle, should it come to that. He drops his chest and peers over the lip. There he is, or the thinning crown of the dude's head anyway, recessed a few feet down in the shadows, nest of sodden leaves and pine needles scattered about his shoulders. And here he comes again, like some deranged Whac-A-Mole.

"Peek-a-boo!"

Graham Enders, yes indeed, only some fifteen years younger.

Fox nervously extends his hand, presses his fingers into *warm* flesh. Yes, warm, but not living. Not really. *Christ, what is he?* Not a man, but very man-like. Some kind of animatronic character granted only a short loop-worth of life, only instead of plastic and plush, this one's made of real skin and hair. It even courses with blood. You can see that in the blush of its cheeks, see the result in its visible breath. Back down he, or, yeah, *it* goes.

Fox tosses the shard, readies himself...

And when the imitation Graham-thing springs up again, Fox catches it under the armpits, uses every remaining ounce of his flagging strength to try and drag it from its hole... but the damned thing's... stuck... hung on... something...

Snap! The two go tumbling, splashing into the slop, Graham-thing's heft pinning Fox flat on his back, its sandpaper stubble abrading Fox's cheek with every vicious recoil of its bobblehead.

"Peek-a-boo!" Its breath splashes rank and muggy across Fox's face.

Rape! Rape! He thinks to scream, the way he does every morning in English when Loretta Vasquez sinks those unrelenting fingers into his hair, *somebody help!* But Miss Woolley's not around to roll her eyes and warn, *hands to ourselves.*

He gets leverage underneath the thing's chest, pushes

hard against its suffocating weight. Just when it seems he might be doomed to asphyxiate, the body tips, rolls.

Freed, Fox hurls himself away, into a tangle of fluorescent mycelium yet to fruit, and glancing back, sees with the advantage of a little distance; that thing is but half a man, with legs of shredded sinew clinging to bone, like some kind of big mammalian turtle plucked from its shell.

Fox cries out in horror and launches out of the pit, splashes upstream, not daring to slow until he finally reaches the safety of the culvert, a stone's throw from civilization, and collapses upon the concrete incline, cool air stinging his flaring nostrils, his gulping lungs. "What the hell, what the hell," his newfound mantra. He starts to scramble up the graffitied pavement when he realizes—

My jacket!

Leave it. Suit's ruined anyway. Go get Pete.

Okay, but I can't just leave Mr. Enders. What if he's hurting?

Hurting? What the fuck even is he?

Fox picks up his coat, dusts it off, puts it on, and steps up to the crater, hands trembling at his face. That thing just keeps giggling and repeating itself, cheery as can be, seemingly oblivious to its condition, and to Fox's presence.

Fox deliberates a while before working up the courage to drop back into the pit. "Hey," he says, and prods it with his foot.

Nothing.

"Are you okay? Do you need help?" He peels the thing's lip back, exposing the damp teeth and gums. So lifelike. So human. So not. He pinches the nose—

"Peek-a-boo!" Graham honks, all stuffed-up.

"No way." Neon tendrils are already webbing, rerouting from Graham-thing's torn up skeleton legs, seeking new connection to the earth... to the burrow from which it was plucked. Just *imagine* what else could be down there.

Fox draws his phone from his pocket, turns on the flashlight, and shines the beam into the shadows, revealing a revolving 3D kaleidoscope—or churning mandala—of mutating trinkets and baubles, all poppling out of each other, and dissolving like stray wisps of fog where their individual transmutations carry them too far from the walls. Fox stands in gape-mouthed awe, his own brand of mimicry.

How can this be?

Several feet down, the darkness is absolute, impenetrable, even by his flashlight. Staring beyond the event horizon, into the yawning void, Fox can almost imagine it calling to him—

Come on in. Know you wanna. Come look. Come see.

Curiosity's always been an irresistible motivator for him. It's what drove him to jam a paperclip into the wall socket by his locker one morning, seventh grade, hanging with Pete, waiting for first bell (no dummy, he held the clip with the rubber soles of his shoes so as not to be electrocuted), a spur of the moment experiment that resulted in a fountain of sparks, a melted outlet, and a power outage for that wing of the school. Curiosity's likewise the force that drove him to begin testing the waters with Ethan, infinitely more dangerous than the wall's measly 120 volts, or so it felt at the time. It was Fox who started them down that road, with all his little touches, whispers, massages. Experiments of a kind. He never meant to toy with Ethan, but fascination compelled him, and before he knew it, he'd charged the air between them.

No, Fox thinks, exercising uncharacteristic restraint. *I'm fine up here, thank you.*

But the ground begins to vibrate beneath his feet, subtly at first, then seismically, and before he can even think to leap away, he's swallowed into the madness.

FOUR
INTO THE KALEIDOSCOPE

ox comes to, wheezing, facedown in a pool of light, some metallic stench burning his nostrils, wet cerulean clay vibrating so fiercely underneath him as to tingle the very molecules of his being. His left arm screams for attention, cranked sharply under his belly. He rolls his weight to his right shoulder, frees it. All around him, neon friendship fibers stand up from the muck like bristling hairs and strain to meet his touch, whether drawn to his presence, or simply his static charge. Fox hovers his hand just above the surface, splays his fingers, flirting with their tickling caress.

He pushes up and rears onto his knees, shields his eyes from the lone shaft of day spotlighting him through the cavern's gaping maw some nine, ten feet overhead. Fluorescent mycelium branches outwards from that rippling esophagus and its tract of blossoming things, fans into the shadows, weaving a complex web overtop a constellation of those crawling stars.

Fox casts his head about, panning for his cell phone, finds it just out of reach, flashlight-down. As he stretches toward it, he notices a mat of blue threads springing up from the dyed earth. Not the same turquoise faux fur from the crater above, but a deeper, darker cobalt blue, and coarser. A well-worn carpet.

The sound of crackling wooden boards draws his attention and the focus of his flashlight beam overhead, where a giant lotus-like bud unfurls five long petals, or, rather, ceiling fan blades, and a frosted glass pod surges with clouds of gaseous phosphorescence that flood the subterranean lacuna with a pulsing amber glow, flaring intensely enough at its brightest intervals to sting Fox's retinas. He folds a limb across his face, buying his pupils time to constrict.

He drags himself to his feet and pockets his phone, flashlight no longer of use. Easing his arm from his eyes, he finds himself in a chamber roughly the size and shape of Ethan's bedroom. In fact...

That's it exactly. Ethan's bedroom, if it had been crudely chiseled out of stone, and then painted and carpeted. The weathered walls bleed multi-pigmented Rorschach blots that coalesce into recognizable images (rock stars mostly, Björk and Kate Bush among others) and take on a filmic sheen, then peel at their edges from the pockmarked plaster, asserting their independence as individual posters, born of stone. All around, such births are taking place, a garden of furniture and teenage clutter flowering from fluorescent mycelium, bringing the bedroom to blossoming life and overtaking that metallic stench with the more potent aroma of skunky weed smoke.

"I got it, I got it, how about Tatiana's Tutu?" Fox whirls at the sound of that squeaky voice. He recognizes it instantly, the barely pubescent squawking of—

His own fourteen-year-old self, slightly sunburned, damp boardshorts saturating the tail of his old Toy Machine t-shirt, lying belly-down atop the plush bedspread, raking his fingers to spike the blue fur, then combing the cowlicks flat again. Beyond him, bleeding inkblots tattoo the wall with a sparser rendition of Fox's mural-in-progress.

Pete's here too, just barely fifteen, tank top, beach towel 'round his waist, cross-legged on the carpet below, smoking weed from a crumpled and perforated Coke can. He bursts into a fit of giggles, clouds jetting through his nostrils. "No way, man."

"Why not?" that young Fox challenges, just as serious as he could possibly pretend to be.

"*Um*," Fox—the *real* Fox—starts to say, and then clamps his trap shut, lest these—*what even are they?*—turn on him. But, like Graham Enders above, they seem oblivious to his presence. He chokes down the excessive saliva drowning the back of his throat, hangs his hands from the lapels of his soiled suit jacket, and throws his gaze to daylight, torn between figuring a way to climb to freedom or placating his increasingly undeniable curiosity.

"You really wanna be in a band called Tatiana's Tutu?"

Fox's young double buries his face in the fur, struggles to contain his giggles. "Definitely."

The flappy sole of Fox's sneaker claps at his heel as he cuts across the craggy carpeted topography for a closer look. Nearer the boys, he can smell the chlorine wafting off them.

He remembers this night well. It was the first time they ever got Ethan to smoke pot. They had just been to Ross Powell's pool party, where this band of sophomores and juniors calling themselves Skull Fuck Blues had played, slayed, and inspired the boys to form a band of their own.

Staying the night at Ethan's afterwards, they started planning, dreaming. Pete already knew how to play guitar (a few chords, anyway). Ethan, bass. *Cool,* so Fox would sing and they'd find a drummer later on or just let a laptop do the job. All they needed was a name, and since no one else was forthcoming with any ideas, Tatiana's Tutu stuck. Fox even designed a logo, *T22,* that went all over everything he owned. The band lived through one practice. Fumbled around on their instruments for fifteen, twenty minutes, went for a snack break, and that was that. Lovely memory, but why, *how* is it here, playing out as some kind of, *uh,* corporeal echo?

Fox clears his throat, "Hello?"

With a sudden *swish* and what could only be described as a physical jump cut, the boys launch back to the top of the memory, the jolt scattering Pete's smoke in swirls. "I got it, I got it, how about Tatiana's Tutu?"

Fox startles backwards, fumbles his footing against the uneven terrain, and thuds ass and elbows into a thinning patch of carpet, mashing the fibers and imprinting his form into the saturated substrate. The shock inspires a rumble of tectonic activity. A rift flares from his contact points. He rolls to get away, but the ground shears, rends open a trench three feet deep, stratified into layers of cerulean, periwinkle, and robin's egg, filling with icy groundwater, into which Fox tumbles, splashes, stirring up clouds of indigo sediment.

Regathering his wits and his appendages, he climbs, dripping, from the gorge and its glacier-blue gush. Accounting the damage, he finds the room graded towards the fault, which strikes out from under the bed, oxbows around Pete, and bores its exit through the far wall, directly under the closet. The burbling waters, there thigh-deep and gated by the latched door, roil and somersault, pile and spill out over the undercut banks, making a marshland of the surrounding carpet.

The ground quakes with a violent aftershock, and Fox's eyes flash with terror as he imagines it all breaking open to greater depths. He flings himself onto the bed, and shelters there, shivering, until the tremors subside.

"That was close," he says, chuckling, relieved, and then realizes with a sudden chill to whom he speaks. He's practically mounted his own double, hand resting on the small of its back, knees compacting the mattress, tipping the thing's weight, so that Fox can feel its ribs resting against his own thighs. "Hey," he says, softly, uncertainly, drawing his hand from it. The poseur doesn't respond. Nor even do its eyes acknowledge Fox's presence. No flit of reflex to track him in their periphery.

"You really wanna be in a band called Tatiana's Tutu?" Pete repeats, head and shoulders cresting over the horizon of the mattress.

"Yo, Pete."

Nothing.

"Hey!" Fox shouts, and spanks his own double's ass viciously enough to set every nerve in his hand ablaze. He hisses and clutches his wrist, palm screaming, "Why, señor, why?"

That thing stifles a giggle, face buried in the pelt. "Definitely," it says, demonstrating either a complete lack of pain receptors or the world's greatest poker face. Then, with another swishing, grating restart, the memory plays again. "I got it, I got it, how about Tatiana's Tutu?"

Fox hooks the waistband of his double's damp boardshorts, yanks to discover its ass cheeks glow fiercely, blood gathering under the surface. Still, the thing registers neither pain nor modesty, at least none that Fox can discern.

The hell, man?

He releases the elastic band. *Snap!*

But wait, so... if Pete and I are here... that means Ethan should be...

There.

And there he is. *There he is.*

Just fourteen years old, slouched in a beanbag chair in the corner, all hibiscus flowers and summer neons, plucking lazily at his bass guitar (Epiphone Thunderbird), face hidden behind the pale stone visage of one of Fox's custom Halloween masks so that he appears, at first glance, to be another Pete. But that mask's not fooling anyone, let alone Fox.

Sympathetic to the shock of the discovery, the cloud-like luminescence swirling within the ceiling fan dome dims to a stormy sallow-grey haze that bleaches out the scenery.

"Ethan?"

Ethan lolls his head. *Does he hear?*

Fox climbs over his own double, legs quivering as he sets foot to carpet and lurches across the stream.

There he is. By whatever magic. Available to touch, to hold, to wrap in his arms and never, ever let go.

"Hey?" Fox drops to his knees, takes the mask by the chin and gently lifts Ethan's gaze, but those eyes, so beautiful, peer through him. "E?"

Fox picks at the edge of the mask. No offense to Pete, but his is not the face Fox wants to see. Maybe not, but the mask is stuck, suctioned to Ethan's face. Fox finds purchase with his fingernails, and very slowly, very carefully, peels—

The mask fights, clings by, what an inch of separation

exposes to be, tensile tendrils of mucus, sinew, gristle, crawling with translucent-white cockroach nymphs, nested in warm wet paradise. Fox cries and releases his hold. The mask—no, actual face—sucks back into place. *Slurp!*

That thing's not Ethan.

As Fox staggers to his feet, the scene resets anew, an effect so violently jarring, so increasingly unnerving, every cord of his neck snaps taut enough to tear. Hunched, grinding his teeth, he tunes to a sound like, what, roaring plumbing? Or a muffled waterfall? *How deep does this all go?* Fox throws his gaze once again to that disc of daylight overhead, edges eaten by its revolving fringe of shapeshifting bullshit.

How am I gonna get out of here?

Scanning the room, he finds salvation in the dresser. Too heavy to drag, but he manages to walk it out from the wall, swinging its weight from one corner to the next. He centers it directly under the spotlight, makes steps of the drawers and climbs to the top, which takes his head and shoulders up into the churning mandala. Tiptoes lift his outstretched arm to within near-reach of the surface.

See ya later, alligator. But one last glance before he goes, down his cocked shoulder at that freak in the mask. And seeing him there—so alone, as Ethan always somehow seemed to be, even in the presence of others—Fox finds himself unexpectedly overcome by affection. Maybe that's not his Ethan, but it is *an* Ethan. And, so wait a minute.

If this place is recreating memories, what else does it have to show? Maybe the day they met? Or the first time they held hands? What if—*what if*—his Ethan's here, somewhere? If he is, Fox has to find him, if only to hug him once more. If only to beg him to live.

He hops back down, and the captive phosphor cloud flares overhead, as if glad for it. He follows the stream to the closet, skids down the ramp of the fault, and wades into the Arctic waters. He plants a foot against the incline, reaches up for the wobbly knob, hesitates, then drags the door against the push of the surge.

The fan's stormy incandescence spills dim and decaying into a lightless zig-zagging fissure, the opening of which resembles giant female anatomy, or so Fox thinks anyway, cut-through with a glacial spring, every bustling inch engaged in tireless reinvention, crisis of indecision concerning its contribution to a perpetually-transfiguring tessellation of—not just bullshit, Fox realizes. These trinkets carry totemic significance. Here on display, a gallery of everything that ever meant anything to Ethan.

Definitely don't go in there, his better judgement begs. The path's narrow enough he can't be certain he won't get stuck. Phone drawn, flashlight triggered, he tells his inner judge where to cram it, then crams himself through the opening and forges sideways into the dark, his left half leading the way.

The path unfurls endlessly from the shadows by stretches equal to his flashlight's throw, but the belongings, they devour light, gobble it into their greedy convolutions, leaving only scraps to glint off rotisserie rubber and cartwheeling plastic. Fox sidesteps his way along, careful, oh so careful, to minimize contact for fear he may too be swallowed—a minute, two—each sloshing step, each further crank of the corridor, more dismayed not to reach some terminus, be it outflow or dead-end (at least then he could turn back, satisfied he'd seen everything).

Near-blindness sets his senses ablaze. Terrible, the

unceasing caresses of those blossoming textures, so unsympathetic to his avoidance. *And, God, what's that smell?* Same noxious metallic stench from before, only now accompanied by the hint of something putrid, fishy, like ground beef packaging left too long in the garbage. The vibration too intensifies, until the entire subterrane throbs like the world's largest sound system, his own body its satellite subwoofer, producing tones so deep they can't even be heard, only felt, a tickling resonance flowing from his core through his extremities. Almost pleasurable, really, just to shut his eyes and let it course through him. Like a full-body massage. Not of tissue, but atoms. Pulsing in waves. As if he'd spent the day at an electric beach and carried the tides home inside him.

Dizzied, Fox tips, scuds spine and shoulders along the wall, feeling its constituents shrivel and involve beneath his touch, then swell and precipitate a confetti of curios too varied to inventory, and moreover too quick in dispersing, extinguishing, evaporating, but of them he tallies: a squirt of electric plasma balls strung wobbling like a quart of water in zero-G that bursts against the opposite wall and scatter-sprays the shadows with tiny lightning-filled gobs; a crackling hail of novelty pop-pops that freeze mid-spark like little flowers of light; a cloud of—oh, the very scent of summer—Kool Aid powder, strawberry kiwi, that settles over the waters in a film of particulate, quickly dissolved, dying the stream punch red. Beyond the tangible comes, issued in that same celebration of contact, a storm of sensation. The fragrance of a freshly-mowed lawn sizzles green and yellow over Fox's taste buds. And is that the sweet, tart tang of a freshly picked blackberry? Playing not on his tongue, but across the phantom sunburn now warming the nape of his neck. A scraped-knee-August-sun-queasiness swells, tumbling into a full-on roller-coaster-gut-gasm.

He doubles over, reaches out to brace himself, and by so doing, inspires further discharge. Another spurt of phosphorescent space fluid—frosted teal this time, rippling surface marred like painted glass by chips and flakes that stretch and run, showing through to irradiated filaments suspended within—splashes slushie-cold across his face and slings off showering the shadows. Blinded, truly now, by strobing splotches of blue afterimage, searing chlorine sting, Fox cries out, folds an arm across his face to protect from further assault, but the onslaught reaches him through other means. Taste, impossible taste, pours into his palms, sour beyond imagining, beyond tolerance. And sound, too, a cacophony, rings not in his ears, but through every vibrating hair on his head. Song birds, a tinkling chime, the flanged roar of a distant plane, the scrape of a metal rake across textured pavement, a boy—is that Fox himself?—laughing; these and a thousand others storm his scalp, imaging by echolocation their conflicting geographies, deranging him so entirely, he loses left from right, up from down, even—he panics to realize—inside from out. He shifts focus to touch, scours every misfiring impulse for his surface, finds it crawling, flowing about him, finds a cold-boiling thickness enveloping him to the waist, and realizes he's fallen to his knees.

Christ, he's fucking losing it, fucking—if only Pete was here, if only Ethan. "Come out of your head," Pete would say; "It's okay, I'm here," Ethan. And finally the tears come, and plentifully, in a fit of sobs. Because for the first time in days, Ethan doesn't feel so impossibly far away. Because he is, isn't he—here? Somehow? In every inch of this place. His record, imprinted upon the earth. Sowed by his blood.

The tempest breaks, draws back its waves. Fox peels his stinging eyes, the very act of which reconstitutes reality (or this peculiar subterranean unreality anyway) and re-individuates him from it. He unfolds his arms from the back of his head, mops the tears from his cheeks, snot from his upper lip.

Fuck was that? Easily a hundred times more intense than his first-last-only time tripping on shrooms, night his dad died. Ages it took to recover from that. If ever he did. So, what, the cave produces its own psychedelic effects? But delivers them how, by blue-light baptism? Osmosis? Is that the aim of the vibration, to churn his body into a psychotropic microbrewery? And how long will he be made to suffer for *this* trip? How many months, years triggered by every quirk of the mind, every bout of déjà vu, fearing he lost his way and blundered out to the wrong reality, where his dad, and now Ethan, are dead instead of alive as they ought to be, and he forever helpless to get back to them; fearing—*Christ*—fearing he never found his way out at all. But this. Maybe this is a madness he could get behind. A madness of Ethan to be swept up and carried off into.

Something seizes upon the exposed flesh between his socks and pant legs, grasps at his ankles. Fox fumbles, almost drops his phone. He casts its light down through the pulling webs of foam, through the curtains of refraction, fearing jellyfish, fearing the spawn of Cthulhu—

Just a snare of friendship seaweed. He reaches down to untangle himself. Weird, but do those woven tendrils—four, plus a fifth opposing—resemble a spaghettified hand? And do they now grip his own?

No, he decides, after a time. They're only animated by the current.

Back up and pressing on, then, only for something oily to drag his neck. Revolting from its touch, he thrashes, pinballs, and finds himself face-to-face with Trent Reznor, perfectly manifested from the "Perfect Drug" video, crowning through the kaleidoscopic weave, screaming nonsense about gregarious blood.

A little girl's shriek comes wailing out of Fox, and he bops the fucker on his nose, sends Trent recoiling back into the patchwork. *Shit, sorry, dude, didn't mean to. Think you're pretty cool, or whatever. First two albums, anyway.*

Just as Fox lowers his defenses, Bjork telescopes over his shoulder, chrome fluids and floral flourishes flowing about her face, singing "Hidden Place."

Fox picks up the pace, his haste stirring a violent slosh that claps hard at the walls and throws up arcs of ice water twice as tall as the torrent is deep.

Light ahead. A haze of aquamarine so anemic as to be outshone even by the crackles still playing across Fox's seared retinas. But the light persists, and glows brighter, its source as yet unglimpsed beyond the turns of the corridor. And not just light but warmth. Sticky, sweltering warmth.

Fox races on, encouraged, the spot of his flashlight whipping every which way.

Then, abruptly and without warning, the path veers sharply to the left, and flares open.

Fox stamps his brakes, teeters on the slick precipice of an alien grotto, large as the Pantheon, rapids gushing around his calves, threatening to wash him over a thirty-foot drop into a luminous swimming hole below, the broad source of the radiance.

He secures his footing, cops a maniac grin, already imagining the reaction Pete and Ethan will—

Oh. Yeah. Shit.

How is it he keeps forgetting, even though it's the only thing he seems capable to think? Milky eyes, skin so cold, those horrible wheezes. That's Ethan now, he has to keep reminding himself. *But yeah, E would totally love this.*

So, okay, details. The cliff the water's pouring over? A crag of palpitating Ethan totems. The pool? Half-Olympic, spanning the chamber's diameter but for a crescent shelf of star-shaped, furred boulders not unlike Ethan's throw pillows. Gentle waves lap at a small beach of multicolored sand carved by branching tributaries of incandescent magma that flow into the lagoon and erupt sizzling into towering columns of steam. Another echo of Graham Enders stands at the shore with a pool skimmer, panning for... *what are they?* Not leaves, but pages of something, floating all over the surface. Craning over the edge, Fox sees that directly below, there's a clone of Ellie, only five, six times larger, a giant in a bathing suit and sunglasses, lounging under the falls with a supersized pulp paperback. *Whoa, cool, hey, Ell—*

Motherfuck!

Something molten streaks the back of Fox's hand and sticks. He hisses, scratches, rakes his nails through a stamp of neon wax. Overhead, in lieu of stalactites: a hanging forest of drip-stick-candle spires, each with a sputtering flame.

Plenty of ambient light here, so Fox holsters his phone and backs himself over the edge, begins to negotiate his way down the slippery, ever-evolving crag, finding a foothold in some blooming void, handhold in a tangle of nickel-wound vines: bass-guitar-strings that sound Eb, D, C upon being plucked. *Shit, man. Whoa.* Peculiar vertigo. Look down, see it all telescope. Bye-bye beach. He tries to focus on the climb, but his left hand recedes to a pinpoint, right hand balloons. *Let go, let it float you.* The image sets him a'gigglin'. Big-ass fist for a hot-air craft, carry him out over the waves. *My god, I'm so ripped.*

Yet, he climbs without incident, and shouts and shouts all the way at Giant Ellie, over there chillin' under the waterfall, his damndest for a grin, a glance, *something*, "Elliiieeee!" but she's even more aloof than the real deal.

Close enough to touch bottom (or is he?—hard to tell when it keeps running to infinity), he reels out a recon unit.

Fox to Team Taffy Toes, come in Taffy Toes, what's the condition on the ground? Is there any? Over.

Proceed with caution, sir. It's a real swampland down here. Over.

Roger that. Stepping off now.

His floppy-soled sneaker scatters a thicket of cold fog, squishes down next to its pioneering counterpart, atop the pile of five-pointed boulders that constitute the crescent ridge, all carpeted by a furry blue algae, slick as a shampooed bathtub, sodden with sea spray, foamy lashes of which spank the star-cleaved rock shelf and cut slithering retreats through geometric crevices, drawing pebbles and shell fragments along. And in those trenches, Fox sees, as clearly and intimately as if down on his knees with a magnifying lens, scuttling skull troopers, same as marched upon the flowering vines above ground, tiny replicas of those hung in his bedroom. But why should his skulls belong to Ethan's world?

Unless he's the one who acquainted Ethan with death.

He drives that sickening thought from his mind.

His present grounding gradually dampens the wilder

perceptual distortions, reduces the cave's effect to a shimmering body high. Seeing more clearly, he casts his gaze up, to the summit of his climb, and swoons, aghast to find a distance of perhaps only fifteen feet. So, wait. His perspective was altered, then, from above? Or could the cliff's actual physical dimensions depend upon angle of view, so that the same distance descending would measure only half in ascent? If you jumped, then, would you fall thirty feet, or fifteen? Pure speculation on Fox's part, but he figures, yeah, no doubt thirty; return climb, fifteen. Something to maybe test with a tape measure. Anyway, from this vantage, Ellie rises a far less impressive ten feet from where she's swallowed at the waist by the luminous waters and by a shroud of rainbowing mist that billows up off the boil of the falls. The lagoon itself: less Olympic, more—well, look, it's still bigger than the neighborhood pool.

Fox plots the way forward. The shelf tapers along the perimeter, crumbles in places to no more than a few outcropping inches. Only route to the beach, save a swim. He shakes off the intoxication, presses himself against the varicolored wax flowstone, and toes his way around, very careful of his step.

Close enough, he leaps ashore (*ouch*, his knee), kicking sand into a lava stream, making it roil and hiss.

Pete is gonna flip. His. Shit.

He wipes the perspiration from his forehead. Warm and humid down here in the lava's orange radiance. Steamy. But, *strange*, the whole right side of his face is burning cold.

Oh, huh. It's the light put off by all those frosted blue Christmas bulbs up there, the ones poppling and crackling, in and out of pockets of erosion all along the undulous grade that flows ceiling into wall. *Cold Lights.* Frost forms on everything caught in their glow.

Fox's attention is drawn back to the swimming hole as Giant Ellie turns a page of her enormous book, overwhelming the grotto with the scent of damp pulp, then adjusts the fold of her leg and sends a pulse of waves to slap at the beach, where Ethan and Ellie (he, eight; she, eleven, to guess) build a sand castle, their joyous giggles fogging the air. Such an incredible thing to see him smiling again, even if long before Fox knew him.

Dropping to his knees next to them, Fox sees that a touch of teal luminescence falls across young Ethan's cheek. Ice crystals flourish there. *No, no. Keep off him.* Fox thaws the child's face with his thumb. *There ya go, buddy.*

For now. But the Cold Lights still shine upon him.

Closer to the water now, Fox can make out what's on the floating pages ol' Graham's been scooping with his net. Pornography. Printed from the web. Anime, mostly. You know the shit. Gay sex as fetishized by horny teenage girls, which means cutesy big-eyed cartoon boys fucking cutesy big-eyed cartoon boys.

Whoa, weird. Didn't know he was into this shit.

Fox reaches into the water (warm, he notes, heated by the lava that feeds into it), grabs one: cutesy big-eyed cartoon boy on all fours, ass propped towards the viewer, pleading expression cranked over his shoulder, *lots* of twinkles in the eyes.

Fox goes off giggling. *Oh my god. How could you even jack off to this?*

Giant Ellie turns another page. *Wonder if she'll ever reach the end of the book? Or maybe the pages just keep refilling.* Part of him wants to swim out to her, climb up her body and find out. But there's plenty else to explore. And more than anything, he just wants to find a fifteen-year-old Ethan. One with a face.

Back to his feet...

Tracking the boundary of the grotto, he finds an inlet, lightless and drawing breath. The very moment he steps up to it, a metallic calamity telescopes way back into the shadows, as if nothing had existed in them before, but Fox's exploration has excited the cavern to cobble together more memories. He draws his phone, reignites its flashlight and enters.

Scent of sweat and rubber, hint of piss. Sticky concrete floor (clings to Fox's shoes, releases with peeling squeaks), a number of puddles (constant drip-drop), wooden benches, rows of lockers (lots of little holes to air the stink out). Panning with the beam, Fox spotlights boys slathering deodorant under their arms (scent of Old Spice) and changing out of gym clothes, pupils gleaming, reflecting, like those of feral cats.

"Get a good look?" Fox knows that voice. Belongs to this asshole Cam Ford, one grade up. Ex lacrosse player, kicked off the team for hazing freshmen. Ended up in Fox and Ethan's gym class last year. Delightful. Fox finds him with the flashlight, a full-grown man, at least compared to the boys gathered around him. "Hey, you hear me? I'm talking to you."

"What?" A mousy, high-pitched voice. Fox lights its owner. Ethan, fourteen passing for twelve, trying desperately to mind his own business as he finishes dressing. Fox gasps, amazed by how young he looks. Just a baby when they met, a year ago. Fox knocks his head against a cool locker. He knows this memory too.

"I said, did you get a good look?"

"No."

"Well, here, let me show you." Cam whips his ugly dick out. "That what you wanna see?"

"No."

"Then why you lookin' at it?"

"I'm not."

Cam lunges, pins Ethan by the neck, bouncing his head off the lockers.

Fox could swear that Ethan's looking directly at him, begging for help. But he's looking at the Fox of the memory, who the real Fox hadn't even noticed, standing within arm's reach, in front and a bit to the side of him, too afraid to intervene.

"Keep your eyes to your fucking self in the locker room," Cam hisses, spraying Ethan with spit, eyes shining murderously in the bounce of Fox's beam, pointed now at the wet concrete, Fox too agonized to bear witness.

He turns from Ethan's pleading eyes, focuses instead on the back of his own fourteen-year-old head, fist balled so tight, his fingernails cut his palm. *Do something, you fucking coward, fucking do something!*

Finally, Cam releases Ethan and the scene rewinds.

If only, *if only*, Fox could change it. But it's done, set in time. Onward, he follows an intensifying fragrance, like fresh rain on dry earth, or the smoky approximation achieved by petrichor-flavored incense, the scent Ethan always burned (rain-lover that he was), especially when Fox and/or Pete would stay the night, written in nonsensical cursive contrails that lead through the lockers to the place where the showers should be. Instead, tiles scatter into another presentation of Ethan's bedroom carved from stone.

Here, the dome-confined tempest radiates a dim heat-lamp orange. The carpet, suffering a severe case of alopecia, sprouts the wispiest tufts from the cerulean clay, here so boggy that Fox sinks nearly to his knees upon entry. In the open center of the floor, where the sludge is especially soupy, bubbles gurgle and burst, expelling puffs of petrichor.

Upon the bed, underneath Fox's mural—here extruded into a three-dimensional bas relief—Fox and Ethan, manifested from a not-too-distant memory, each pretend to watch the lame horror movie playing on the laptop between them, but each is actually acutely focused on the other, because they're holding hands for the first time.

"Is this okay?" Ethan asks.

Upon spotting them, Fox vents a quivering lament. Teardrops skate his cheeks. "Ethan," he manages, hardly more than a whimper, to no reply.

His legs give, drop him into the quicksand with a horrid aching bellow more likely to have issued from an aggrieved elephant than a boy. He grips handfuls of hair at the crown of his head and rocks himself sobbing. "Ethan," he tries again, with the faintest of hope. "Ethan, please." *Please say something. Please do something. Please just don't be fucking dead.*

"Is this okay?" Ethan repeats.

Yes, Fox thinks, and stops rocking. But his memory-self seems burdened, uncertain.

Fox tows himself up out of the sludge and trudges forward, leaving a trail of burbling burrows as he goes, goop sucking at his every step. He's nearly to the boys when the bog slurps the shoe from his trailing left foot. Fox cringes as his wavering balance forces him to plant his socked toes into the mush. He rolls up his sleeve, fishes the sneaker out, tosses it to dryer ground, *splat*, nearer the locker room. He tosses the other one too, preemptively, and his socks, then hoists himself onto the bed. He knocks the computer away and straddles Ethan's lap, trembling to examine his lover up close.

"Is this okay?" Ethan asks again, dizzying Fox's senses with his cool spearmint breath.

"Yes."

He may be a memory, but he's solid. And warm. *Christ, so warm.* Fox combs his muddy fingers from Ethan's temple, 'round back to his crown, and gently brings their foreheads together.

With closed eyes, he shudders. "Please, Ethan. I was only kidding. You have to know I need you." He presses their lips together for the first time, not counting that horror at the creek.

He backs away, eyes easing open, lips silently repeating, *please, please...*

Nothing.

He's not sleeping beauty and he's not going to live again.

"Ethan," Fox says more sharply, grasping a handful of the thing's shirt. "Wake up!" His roar echoes throughout the cavern.

Fox returns from the earth, air-dried tears sticky on his cheeks. He stumbles, spinning from the crater, clings to a tree by the stream, a ghastly sinking void in his chest where had been vibration, weariness where every cell had been thrilled. As he gradually readjusts, he distinguishes another sensation too, an odd sort of discomfort. Hunger. Overcome by astonishment as he had been, he hadn't noticed it creeping up on him.

God, that petrichor. Still heavy in his nostrils, lungs. No, wait, that's the real thing. Looking up, he sees dark clouds rolling in. A drop streaks his cheek, then another, and soon enough, it's pouring.

FIVE

PSYCHIC BRINE

Rain boils over Pete's skylight. He lies below, watching, contemplating, toying with the BB Fox long ago planted in his belly (oh, the marks friends make), rolling it under the flesh. He came up after the service, thought he might try and sleep a while, but he's too scared to let himself drift. When he does, the nightmares come. The ones where he finds Fox out by the creek, gone by Ethan's example.

His phone lights up on his night table. Summer, most likely. He promised he'd call after the service, but he hasn't yet. She keeps asking if he wants to talk about it and telling him it's okay to cry and all that well-meaning shit, and he just can't deal with all that expectation right now.

The doorbell rings. Moments later, Pete's dad calls for him, so Pete slips into a pair of jeans and heads down.

"He's really upset," Dad says. "He wouldn't come in."

Pete finds Fox on the porch, suit soaked and muddy, eyes puffy and red.

"Hey? You okay?"

Fox dawdles, pulling at a sprung thread.

"Why you all muddy?"

"I have to show you something."

"What?"

"Just come and see, okay?"

"You've been at the creek?"

Fox nods, anguished.

Why would you ever, ever go back there?

"There's no way I can explain. You just have to see. Just come, okay?"

Pete relented, grabbed his hoodie and a slice of cold pizza for Fox, then they went around to the garage and got the eight-foot aluminum stepladder (that part took considerable convincing). Now they're lugging it together through the drizzle, winding it through the trees, Fox half-expecting to find everything all sealed up, to find he only imagined it.

You need to come home.

Those words, like weather-portending scar tissue, herald the image. Branded upon Fox's brain in a single blistering glimpse, more potent, more damaging than a peek at the sun, through the front door, beyond his mother's shoulder before she could move to intervene, what had been his dad. And with the image returns that terrible, gnawing suspicion. What if, *what if*, he never found his way back? Not to *his* reality, where Dad was as he should have been. Alive. God, how that notion plagued him. He would have lost himself to that lunacy if it hadn't been for Ethan and Pete and their constant reassuring presence, grounding him to the present. Escaping out here with them meant everything.

But maybe I am crazy.

If so, then Pete is too. Arrived at the portal, it inspires in him the same slack-jawed mimicry it had in Fox. Pete drops his end of the ladder. "Oh shit, Fox, what happened to him?"

"Nothing."

"Mr. Enders?" Pete leaps into the crater (now filling with foamy rainwater) to render aid. "Call nine-one-one!" he yells, struggling to heave the facedown victim from the flood. "Hang on, we're gonna get help," he says, determined, but then he turns the thing over, and sees finally its big dopey grin—

"Peek-a-boo!"

Fox goes off giggling.

Pete wipes the stinging wet from his eyes and looks up, utterly bewildered. "What the actual fuck?"

"He's not real."

"*What?*"

"See his roots?" Fox gestures to the shapeshifting blooms. "He's just another of those."

Pete takes in the otherworldly vegetation with horror. "What is this? How are you doing this?"

"I'm not doing it. It's Ethan," Fox says, and splashes down into the crater with Pete. "Just look." He drops to his knees before the rain-swallowing mandala.

"The fuck is that?"

"The Sphincter of Madness."

Pete crawls to the edge, peers beyond the poppling totems, into what looks like... Ethan's bedroom? "How can this be?"

"Help me get the ladder."

Fox clanks halfway down the aluminum rungs, then leaps off onto the uneven terrain. *Squish.* The carpet ripples in choppy concentric waves, like water-bloated sod. Pete clambers down to the last step, hooks an elbow and surveys the space, hesitant to dismount, reluctant to set foot upon this world that upends everything he thought he knew about reality. "Dude. I'm tripping the fuck out right now."

"I know."

"How did this happen?"

"It's his blood, man. You can smell it all in here."

Pete's nostrils flare. Yeah, he smells it.

"It's like, he fertilized the mud or something."

Pete spots their clones. The discovery drives him up a rung, with a reinforced grip 'round the rain-slickened rails.

"Come on."

"Is that Ethan?" Pete asks, voice raspy, flared eyes aimed down the barrel of his cocked shoulder at their masked friend below, slouched in a beanbag chair with his bass guitar.

"It all is. This whole place."

The ceiling fan dome flushes warm.

"We shouldn't be down here," Pete says.

"Why?"

"Something's wrong. This isn't right."

"It's fine. Come on."

"No, no. What are those things?"

"It's just a memory. You 'member that night?"

Pete shrugs. He does. But that comforts him little.

"There's all kinds of memories in here."

"But they, like—do they see us?"

"No, s'like Chuck E. Cheese." He demonstrates as much with another assault on his double's ass.

Pete eases himself down. One small step for man...

He tests the bounce of the sod, then crosses to Ethan, gives the thing a curious nudge with his knee. Winning no response, he reaches for the mask—

"Don't!"

"Why?"

"It's..." If Pete sees, he might freak and bail. If it's been anything for him like it has for Fox, then he's struggled enough not to remember Ethan as something gruesome. Better to spare him this. "Just don't."

Pete releases the mask.

Fox cops the impish grin Pete's learned to distrust. "Okay, come on, come on, I call this The Trial of Sanity."

"So you just went ahead and named every fuckin' thing in here."

"Isn't that what cavers do? Don't touch anything." And with that, Fox launches himself into the gauntlet.

They clear the trial without major incident, but Pete's face now. S'what Fox lives for. Those eyes bugging as he takes in the grotto from atop the waterfall. Off to the side, Fox strips to his boxers.

"What you doing?"

"S'not as high as it looks."

"What?" Pete asks, clearly horrified by the thought that Fox might—

Yup, launch himself howling over the edge, epic flying squirrel into the lava-irradiated swimming hole.

Impact yanks Fox's boxers to his knees, plunges him twenty feet to the rocky depths, a simmering shroud preserving his modesty, had he any. He draws his shorts and swims out from the churning boil of the arctic falls, into clearer, warmer waters... and, delight to his salt-stung eyes, discovers a seabed not of rock but ceramic. Here, Ethan's snow globe collection has been reimagined as a majestic coral reef, ceramic bases fused into a craggy pictorial topography from which squishy domes blossom to meet Fox's presence, fibrillating like jellyfish, pumping their contained particles into tiny flurries. Hosted inside the globes, and illustrated all across the reef in a bas relief panorama that would shame even Bosch by its sheer scope and intricacy: the story of Ethan's life.

Paddling close, that he might better appreciate its detail (if only he had thought to bring goggles), Fox is tickled pink to find depictions of the time they shredded Pete's garbage can with a sparkler bomb... and the time they toilet-papered Cam Ford's house, a job so thoroughly done you couldn't even see in from outside the fringy white veil... and the time they rearranged the letters on the sign out front of Ethan's neighborhood, so that Tall Pines read Tall Penis.

Out of breath, Fox kicks off, jets to the surface, breaches through the paper debris, into the fine icy mist drifting off the falls and the sparse pitter-pattering drizzle not of water but neon wax, splatting off the drip stick stalactites and congealing on contact, dotting the waves with Crayola lily pads.

"The fuck, bro?" Pete's voice echoes down in a slow cascade of piling layers. Very trippy. Very not happy.

"What?" Fox giggles, shakes out his hair, wipes his eyes.

"Thought you died, dude."

"How long was I in the air for?"

"Didn't know I was s'posed to count."

"You're always s'posed to count air." Fox hoovers a mouthful of water, shoots it through the little gap in his teeth. Salty. His eyes explode open. "It's psychic brine! I'm swimming in it!"

"The hell does that mean?"

"That band I sent you. They should do a video down here! Be so dope."

"S'it cold?"

"Nuh-uh. Warm. Really warm."

"Liar."

"Not lying." *Oh yeah, shit, but all this porn. Probably should have helped Mr. Enders scoop it out before I brought Pete. Whatever. I've jacked off to weirder shit than this.* "C'mon!"

Pete hems and haws above, then begrudgingly unpacks his pockets (phone, wallet, Altoids).

Fox has always held sway over Pete. Not that Pete's some perfect angel—not by any stretch—but too many times he's played Fox's shadow and followed well beyond his limits into whatever mess Fox happened to cook up, and more often than not paid some kinda price for it. But Pete's more reluctant to just follow into this madness, to dive in with both feet, as Fox very literally has. Now here he stands, on the brink, with Fox for a tour guide, God help him.

He strips to his jeans and begins his descent, keys jangling from the carabiner hooked to his belt loop.

"You're not gonna jump?"

"No way, man."

"Why not?"

"Don't really feel like dying today."

"You're not gonna die."

"Yeah, I know, 'cause I'm not gonna jump." But then he does jump, albeit from a much more manageable height. Showy dismount, hard landing atop the slick, algae-coated surface of the star-cleaved rock shelf, sending its shroud of cold fog swirling. He glances up, as if to commemorate the accomplishment, then, not believing his eyes, whips his head around for a double take.

"Told you, it's not as high as it looks."

Pete turns from the bluff, hand held up to censor it from his view. "This is so fucked." He presses himself against the wax flowstone and begins toeing his way around the narrow ledge to the beach.

Fox slings water. "Don't slip."

"Stop. Fox, stop, I'm serious," Pete says, although his laughter says otherwise.

"Are you even gonna get in?"

"What difference does it make?"

"It makes a lotta difference."

Pete leaps into the sand, checks out a lava tributary, spits into it. "Feels fucking weird in here, man. You feel it? Like, I feel like I keep flowing off this way." He holds his left hand out to demonstrate.

"Feels like tripping." Fox clings to the edge of the pool, where, encouraged by his contact, new textures propagate. Among them, a series of jagged ossified thorns. Shark teeth.

"I guess." Pete draws his vape from his pocket, takes a fat rip. "But, like, a bad trip, if anything."

Fox snorts. "Why's it bad?"

"Just the feel of it."

"I like it."

"You would."

That sobers Fox. It's what Ethan always used to say.

"Swear to God, too, I can almost taste with my skin."

"And hear with your hair."

"Yes, dude! Really, you got that too? 'Cause I thought I was goin' insane."

"We should bring some orange juice in here," Fox says. Word is, that can amplify a trip.

"You don't have to turn everything up to eleven, man. It's intense enough." Pete cuffs his jeans over his knees and follows the lava from dry sand to mushy, lets a wave wash over his toes. "It really is warm," he says, teeth chattering from the Cold Light falling over his bare torso.

"Wasn't playin' no tricks."

"Thought you was."

"No sir, not me."

"Alright, then."

"So, you gettin' in or what?"

Pete takes another hit, tosses the vape into the sand, along with his keys, then dives under the pornography-strewn surface.

Something tickles Fox's leg. *Don't*, he giggles, squirms, kicks, suspecting Pete intends to dunk him... but Pete surfaces way over there by the waterfall. *So, what was...*

Fox swipes the porn away, clearing his view to the glowing depths. Like crystal, the water, visibility straight to the bottom.

"What is this shit?" Pete peels an explicit anime drawing from his shoulder.

But Fox is preoccupied. Was it simply his imagination?

Some random debris? *Yeah, I guess,* he tells himself, lifting his head and squeegeeing the salt from his eyes. *Don't freak out. It's just, like, trip paranoia. Think happy thoughts. Don't let yourself spiral. Happy thoughts, happy thoughts...* (mental image of Ethan, cold)... *fuck, why can't I think of anything happy?* "Pete?" That just burst out of him, a little too desperate-sounding, *shit.*

"Huh?" He's over there in the rainbowing billows of the aeresolized falls, climbing Ellie's slick torso.

"Nothing."

Pete mounts Ellie's dripping forearm, snatches her giant sunglasses for himself. "How I look?"

"Throw 'em here, I wanna wear 'em!"

Pete flings 'em: *kerplunk!* Fox dives, feet kicking gracelessly, catches up before they hit bottom... reemerges wearing them, plus a big cockeyed smile, and reclines into a floating drift.

"See these?" Pete tosses his head at Ellie's giant breasts, spattered with glittering seaspray.

"So fire."

Pete's grin curls devilish. "Lil' look-see?"

I mean. Only pair Fox ever saw, in person anyway, belonged to this girl Aimee Roethke he dated one week in eighth grade. She'd just pierced her nipples the night before with a safety pin and wanted to show off her handiwork, whipped her shirt tail up right there in the school caf for Fox and about a dozen other unwitting witnesses to behold. They got together and tried to do one of his nipples that weekend. Sterilized a safety pin with a lighter. Numbed the nipple with an ice cube. Got the needle about halfway through (by his account, anyway; the way she tells it, they barely broke flesh) before he started howling and made her stop.

Anyway, yeah, hers were cool, but at this scale, Ellie's are really something, and, yeah, okay, he's curious, but.

Pete tugs the ties.

"Don't."

"Why?"

"That's rape, bro."

"How's it rape? She may as well be a fuck doll."

"I dunno, man. Look where you're sitting on her."

Pete's straddling touch imprints pale marks upon her sunkissed flesh. Seeing so unnerves him. "What, she feels me?"

"Could be."

"Did you not say they were like Chuck E. Cheese?"

"Well, what the hell do I know?" Fox thinks of Ethan in his boggy bedroom, all of a hundred feet away. So lifelike. So warm. So available to hug, hold, kiss, imprint with Fox's every touch. He whimpers inadvertently, covers his mouth. *Oops.*

Pete gets himself cackling. A deranged, lunatic laughter, wholly unprompted, unless by cave-induced high.

"What?"

"This is *seriously* so fucked."

"Yeah."

Pete hangs off Ellie's arm, drops back into the water, and swims out to join Fox in the center of the pool. "How deep does it go?"

"Couldn't be more than twenty feet."

"No, dumbass. The cave."

"I dunno. Prob'ly forever." *At least if it's as deep as Ethan is, or, shit—was.*

Pete blows out his lungs and plunges down, down... into the trenches of the illustrated reef. He settles cross-legged among the pulsating globes, his backside stroked by the cool convolving bleed of the falls, front warmed by the slow fanning fingers of radiant ooze. Delicate harmony. He shuts his eyes, erases everything, claims it his to reimagine, a talent he near-to-mastered as a boy, practiced at the bottom of the neighborhood pool, where staring up with considerable focus through a partition of ripples, he could convince the weather to change, convince even, given tremendous concentration, the very season to change, if only until he breached. He conjures now a dream in which Ethan lives, holds it as long as his lungs will allow...

But reality intrudes, rips him from his seat with a mighty gush of displaced water. His eyes blast open. Is that... *who's yelling?* He kicks to the surface.

"Swim!" Fox screams, utterly goddamn hysterical, from the safety of the beach.

Pete's responding yelp is drowned by a swallow of saltwater as something bumps him.

"Pete, swim!"

Pete thrashes one-eighty and sees an unnaturally colored dorsal fin cutting the waves not ten feet away, circling back around. *Oh fuck.* Dipping under, he sees no ordinary hammerhead, but something rather more like a child's drawing of one come to life: dayglow orange with vivid sky blue tiger stripes (hand-scribbled, it would seem, as if with crayon), mismatched fins, googly eyes, and a serious overbite full of white razors of radically varying sizes. It slows, hovers; its stripes begin to pulse and sweep, giving the impression of electric flesh, of twenty million microscopic LEDs programmed as if for a sick rave. Pete finds himself unable to look away, even as he realizes the display's meant to mesmerize, to incapacitate, even perhaps to induce seizures, in advance of attack.

"Come on!" Fox's muffled cry breaks the spell.

Although usually a strong swimmer, Pete feels himself floundering, panic muddling his natural athleticism, wet jeans dragging him down.

"What are you doing? Fucking, swim!"

I'll kill you, he thinks, just before his arms and legs find their groove and paddle him to land, where Fox welcomes him in, drags him from the water.

"Rawr!" the shark sort of yells unimpressively, with a voice like a child impersonating a dinosaur, as it hurls itself ashore, crawling with disproportionate flippers, strobing shades of rust and rot, punctuated by flares of laser lemon. "Rawr," it shouts again, and busts up giggling as it gobbles after Pete, expelling sulfurous smog-breath.

Fox kicks sand into its eyes, maw. The beast sobs like a hurt kiddo, blazes a feverish red, and wriggles back down the slope into the water.

"What—*the fuck*—was that?"

Fox falls over laughing.

"It's not funny"

"I know."

"I could have been killed."

"*I know*," Fox tries, fails to stifle his giggles.

"Fuck, dude." Pete collapses onto his back, clutches his chest, feeling the powerful kick of his heart.

"I dub this... Shark Bite Beach."

Pete breaks into a grin, flips Fox the finger. "You gonna let me name anything?"

"You can name *it*, you want." Fox cants his head toward the shark.

"Gee, thanks."

"What, I'll name it."

"Go right ahead."

"How 'bout Mr. Fishy?"

"How 'bout not."

"Well, what you wanna call it?"

"You hear its stupid voice? I bet it can talk."

"Pete, no. That's like..." Fox rolls his eyes back, counting... "Ten words. I like Mr. Fishy better."

"Stupid." Pete sits up , rakes the beach for his vape, wipes the sand from the mouthpiece, and plugs his mouth.

"That's different. Than the other night," Fox says, face full of...

"Coffee."

"Oh." Fox hugs his torso, rubs his arms, soaked, shivering in just his boxers.

"How's it so goddamn cold?" Pete says, his own teeth chattering, and not just from the adrenaline crash. Water droplets crystalize about his teal-lit shoulders, turn to ice.

"It's the Cold Lights. Up there. Move out of the blue."

Pete looks up at the poppling teal bulbs, moves out of their shine and into the glow of a molten rock flow.

Fox almost follows, but something about Pete's tone and body language suggests maybe he'd prefer some space. *He probably wishes it was me who died*, Fox thinks, and retreats into his head hole, closes the shutters. Unlike with his mushroom trip, there are no visuals inside, only darkness. He finds the depth at which his sensory organs reside (eardrums in particular), and the manner in which that depth colors inflowing stimuli, greatly magnified by his heightened spatial sensitivity, finds his skull thereby transformed into its own catacomb, adjunct to Ethan's, but utterly void. *Being dead must be like this. Wouldn't be so bad if there was music. I'd go crazy otherwise, just thinking and thinking and thinking. I hope Ethan's not thinking too much. I hope he's not thinking he made a mistake. Or maybe I hope he is, because he should know he fucking—*

"Where are you right now?" Pete's voice cuts through.

Whoa. Fox throws open his shutters. "Man, I was somewhere else for a minute."

"I know, I could tell. Maybe don't think too much. You're gonna freak yourself out." Almost happened with the shrooms. Pete had to take him for a walk, change the scenery to distract him, keep him outside himself. And that was even before the two worst things that ever happened. He's got an infinitely deeper well of darkness to drown in these days.

"I just keep thinking how much Ethan would love this," Fox says and then hugs his folded legs, rests his chin.

"Ethan *lived* this. I mean, right? I really don't think he loved it so much, considering."

Fox's lip quivers; he bites to stop it.

"Sorry. I'm an asshole."

"No, you're prob'ly right." Fox sniffles, wipes his nose on the back of his hand.

"Come over here, man. It's warm."

Fox fights an urge to gush, instead only scoots himself in.

"You really think his blood made all this?"

"Ethan sent me this thing once, this article about some experiment with rats and mazes that, like, proved memories could be passed through generations, like, you know, stored in DNA. So, I've been thinking, what if his DNA, like, sort of seeded the soil or something?"

"That doesn't make any sense."

"Makes sense to me."

"Dude, you're in remedial science."

"Okay, asshole. Just because I'm not in AP, doesn't make me special needs."

"Sorry, but that just doesn't make any sense to me."

"Well, whatever, then. I dunno. Maybe it's just like echoes, you know, like, psychic reverb or something."

"If it's reverb..." Pete pauses, hesitates... "I mean, you know that reverb decays."

The thought hadn't even occurred to Fox until now. What if this doesn't last? He takes up a handful of sand, watches the grains sift and drain through his fingers. "Pete," he sort of gasps weakly, needing very badly, and at the same time not wanting to say, "there's something..." His voice trails off.

"What?"

"There's something in here you're gonna find out if we keep exploring. Something you might not like."

"What do you mean?"

Fox shrugs, pained.

"What're you talking about?"

"I'unno." Fox silently begs Pete not to press him any further, but Pete's not having it—

"Just say it."

"If I show you something, you promise not to freak out?"

"What is it?" Pete asks, far less patient.

"Never mind, just forget it. You wanna go look around?"

They must by now have descended a quarter mile into crisp darkness, through a fissure found far side of the beach, down a gently curving, almost imperceptibly sloping helix graduated by steps of a lumpy, pitted sort, ice-slick, that run fortyfold at least their rise, striped lengthwise by a vein of percolating brine, Pete lighting the way with the scant cast of his keyring LED, Fox bear-hugging his own goose-pimpled torso to quell the violent quaking brought on by exposure, by his decision to traipse half-nude, so loathe was he to drape himself once more in that abhorrent funeral garb. Pete, whose soaked jeans *swish-swish* with every step, wasn't himself too eager to traverse the narrow ledge and risk falling into the shark den, so he's likewise gone shirtless, although he has his coffee-scented vapor and a good bit more muscle to warm him.

Heading out, Fox led Pete away from the wing he had explored earlier, the one that memorializes his cowardice and, more importantly, his secret romance. A part of him really needs Pete to see, to understand just how much he's lost, and how much he's to blame, but he's just not ready yet. Of course, other vaults may out him yet. That'd be okay, though. Kind of ideal, really, like someone else telling Pete for him. God, honestly, what a relief that would be.

But if this path has memories to show, it's yet to produce them. In this corridor, rather, memory substances commingle, as if decomposed and redistributed by trickling water, deposited in overlapping layers such that a fossilized cascade of jack o'lantern wavelets glaze great billowing humps of petrified deck wood; such that crystalized firework sparks flourish like feathery frostwork over potholed asphalt edifices, and similar licks of vitrified flame contour brain-like knobs of calcified wool (argyle and rainbow-striped); such that galvanized steel dribbles off an overhang of playground plastic.

Fox's body throbs to the cave's ever-more sonorous lament. His scalp prickles, his hundred thousand antennae tuned to depths that drip, fizz, sputter, and thwack, as if gushing, coalescing ahead of the boys' arrival to facilitate exploration, to lure them untold depths, lure them perhaps to Earth's very core. And where are they anyway? Surely by now well out from under the woods and the bordering houses. Or did they descend through a rift in spacetime, into some kind of pocket dimension occupying no more volume in sum than its aperture?

"You hear that?"

Pete, moon-eyed with alarm: "What?"

Fox has always been a lightweight. Alcohol, that time on shrooms, even with weed. Susceptible to psychedelic effects Pete could never relate. Just a ridiculously low threshold to intoxication. So it seems here.

"What is it?"

"Nothing." Strange, though, he can sorta see, or sense, beyond the throw of Pete's LED, yards ahead mapped by ultrasound, and so detects well before they arrive at a fork in the path.

"Which way?" Pete's panning beam does little to highlight any obvious pros or cons.

Fox selects on instinct, his sonar likewise failing in that respect. "Right."

But Pete lingers, something to say.

"What?"

"Do you not feel dizzy? Swear I'm so fucking seasick just standing in here."

"No," Fox says, even though, *yeah. Dizzy as a goddamn tornado.* But Pete's not asking that, really. He's asking, *should we turn back.* So yeah, no. Definitely not.

Right said Fred, then... through a tangle of cobwebs, into a memory nested in shadow, into yet another duplicate of Ethan's bedroom, only as it appeared long before these boys knew him. No band posters or cool seventies shit, none of Fox's drawings; instead, bunk beds, toys, etc. Clouded in some fine black effluvia that settles heavy as led in Fox's lungs. Pete fires a salvo of sneezes, each more convulsive than the last. Hiccuping surges of foamy, detergent-scented water slosh through sockets of eroded plaster, wash the particulate from the walls, and cut transparent swirls into the inky, ankle-high groundwater. Ethan's mom (sweatshirt, jeans, wet to the knees) makes the bed. Ethan (maybe three, four years old) splashes up with a gift. "Here, Mommy. This is for you," he says, and hands it over.

Placed in her palm: a quarter machine capsule, cockroach trapped inside. "Ethan," she shrieks, hurls the gift.

"It's still God's creature," Ethan says, pouting.

Pete and Fox crack up, simultaneously echo, "It's still God's creature."

"What a brat," Pete says, laughing.

"You should try that on your mom."

"And be disowned?"

The memory loops back again, and Fox can't help wondering if Ethan knew even then he was gay. He vaguely recalls Ethan telling him they used to go to church when he was a kid, he and his family. So that's Ethan maybe trying to work out opposing sentiments in their faith, before they jettisoned that part of their lives. Or maybe he's just being silly. Who knows?

Pete swipes his finger along the surface of the desk, draws up a cake of charcoal dust. "What is this crap?"

"Ash?"

"Ugh, smell it," Pete says, and thrusts his finger into Fox's face.

"No thanks." Fox swats his hand and retreats.

"Just smell it." Pete advances.

"No, stop!" Fox giggles, thumps the wall, cornered.

Pete lunges, Fox dodges, Pete pursues, tackles him onto his back, into the shallow water.

Fox swallows hard, looking up at Pete, waiting for him to do what he will or won't. Although he doesn't hold a candle to Ethan's beauty (which, more than a nice-looking face, had a million sublayers of nuance and mystery to get lost in), Pete's handsome in his own right, Fox has often thought, but in more the way girls like than the way boys like, or *whatever*, the way *he* likes, anyway, if his opinion even counts. He's thought about it plenty, and there's a lot of stuff he'd be willing to try with Pete that he never would have done with Ethan, only because it would be way less intense, like masturbation, really, only less lonely. But for a brief moment with Pete shirtless atop him, and Fox stripped to his boxers, Fox feels a flutter of that same intensity (albeit in this case one-sided) that would sometimes overwhelm him when alone with Ethan. *What the hell is wrong with me?*

Pete smears the grime all across Fox's lip.

"Get off!" Fox shouts, shoves. No trace of good humor.

"Sorry." Pete climbs off, clearly bewildered.

Fox crunches over his knees, cups water and paws at his face. Whatever that shit is, it's fucking vile.

"Hey, check it," Pete says, from somewhere in the shadows. Fox can see the faint haze of the LED flashlight in his periphery, but he doesn't look.

Swallowed in darkness, he thinks of those Psychic Brine videos and their infinitely appealing rectangular abysses. He can almost pretend he's fallen through and into one of them now. He considers skulking silently into the shadows and simply fading to black. He imagines how Pete would react, discovering he's all alone, how panic would set in gradually, how he'd call and call for—

"Fox."

"What?"

"Check it out. It's your room."

Fox gets up and joins him at a spot where the seam between wall and floor rends open in a kind of cupid's bow fissure, dribbling ink into a cavernous impression of Fox's own skeleton-adorned bedroom some eight feet below, sunken into knee-deep, carbon-dusted waters that gently slosh, throwing Pete's beam back in blinding streaks. All three boys are down there, dimly lit by a dust-blotched television screen, looping a scene from earlier this year, judging by their appearances, although the recollection seems rather unremarkable, seeing as they're only playing video games.

Fox drops in; Pete follows, their splashes unsettling the waters, making waves that slap against the walls.

Memory Pete sits submersed to his chest on the floor against the foot of the bed, controller in hand. Ethan perches over his shoulder, cross-legged atop the bed, playing second controller. Fox reclines against the headboard, spectating (hair much shorter and more orderly then, before he grew it into the chaos he currently sports).

"Dead end," Pete says, unimpressed.

Fox flips the light. Vapors charge flickering into the dome, a faint whoosh of blues and oranges that die with a puttering gasp. He sweeps the flocking from the television screen, freeing its light to spill over the tableau. *Seriously, what is this shit?* Accreting over the furniture, the boys, even the waters. Reminds him of this project they did in his elementary school art class, where they filled a page with swirls of color, covered that in black crayon, and then scratched through the waxy surface, carving pictures that let the rainbow shine through again.

"Let's go up for air, man. I can't breathe," Pete says, voice choked, wheezy.

"You can go."

"You gonna make me go alone?"

"I'm still looking."

"It's a dead end. What else you gonna see?"

Fox wades to the closet, throws open the doors. The bare bulb mounted inside surges with bleach-yellow vapors, and remains lit. Suddenly exposed, several dozen cockroaches disperse. Fox yelps. God's creatures or not, he still loathes the things. The waters below, lapping 'round the cramped cove, whip up swirling bands of froth and shoot dazzling glares off an oily iridescent surface sheen. The porous walls recede well into the depths, and then flare open to an abyss. A few skittering roaches smack onto the choppy surface, where their touch excites microscopic plankton to phosphoresce, discharging radiant splotches of pulsing amber that cool to a dim ultraviolet before extinguishing altogether.

Fox gasps.

"What?"

"Look, look, come here." He plunges his cupped hands into the closet waters, draws up a dripping bowl of noctilucence, and angles his body to eclipse the closet light, so his catch will shine more brilliantly.

"Whoa." Pete, watches, awed as the plasma shifts hues

and decays. "That's lit." He drags his toes through the greasy wash, sketches his own luminous squiggles.

Fox cops a big, dopey grin. Finally something here Pete's into. "Jump in," he says, and then loses it at the withering side-eyed glance Pete casts him. He snags his geometry text off the nearby desk.

"What're you doing?"

"I have an idea, watch." He drops the book into the soup. It plunges like a Catherine wheel, firing shimmering sparks as it streaks to the bottom, maybe fifteen, maybe twenty feet below. "What you think's down there?" Fox flashes the dimple-making side-grin that would have had Ethan leaping in right alongside him.

"No."

"What?"

"I'm not getting back in water."

Fox gestures to Pete's keyring flashlight. "Think it's waterproof?"

"*No, man.*"

"It breaks, I'll buy you a new one."

"Plenty of light." Pete stirs the plankton. "Just flap your arms."

"You serious?"

"Yuh-huh."

"You can't point that like you can a flashlight."

"Do like Miss America, bro." Pete paddles the air, rapid as a hummingbird.

Fox cracks up. "You right. Some shark come grab me out the dark, you'll be glad you kept it."

Pete sighs, offers the keyring in his open palm. Before Fox can take it, he snaps his fist shut. "Please, man. Let's just go up for air."

"After this." Fox works at Pete's grip.

Pete unfurls. "You lose my keys, I'll kill you."

"Thanks, Pee-pee."

Pete rolls his eyes.

Fox shines the beam into the watery void, fills his lungs... releases. Shit. He's a little surprised how nervous he is about it. Maybe Pete's right. Maybe they should just go. He takes another breath, holds... teeters... tips himself forward, slave to impulse. His plunge produces an explosion of light so intense Pete has to throw his arms up to shield his eyes.

As the agitated pool dims to a cooler ultraviolet, Pete lets his blinders down and, seeing through a haze of blazing splotches scorched onto his retinas, curses his buddy's apparent death wish. The roiled waters thrash about the room, break over the bed, drawing Pete's attention to the memory, where that younger Fox taps at Ethan's thigh with his socked foot.

Then the real Fox breaches, treads, igniting fresh blooms of phosphor. "Shit, dude," he says, really broken up about something, "I'm so sorry."

"What?"

"I dropped your keys."

"Ha-ha."

"No, man. For real. I'm really sorry, I dunno what happened."

"Well, go get 'em!"

"It's too deep."

"You fucking serious?"

Fox whips the keys up and strobes the LED rapid-fire at Pete's face.

Pete clenches his eyes, shoots up his middle fingers, kicks water.

Giggle, *thunk*. A sound like a body yanked under. A sound like—

"You didn't just get eaten, right?" Pete eases one eye open, then the other. "Fox?" Pete steps up to the dimming eddy, fully expecting Fox to pop up and grab his ankle, yank him under. But Fox is ten feet down, busy painting light-streaks.

A mattress squeak calls Pete's attention to the memory boys. That younger remembrance of Fox crawls the bed, cups his hand to Ethan's ear. Tickled by the whispering breath, Ethan shrugs, snorts, squirms.

Pete drags his lead foot through the slosh, and thereby triggers a cascade of springy, plasticky clicks from the bedroom's dim perimeter. Television light glances off two dozen glossy orbs. Do Fox's skulls see? Do they track Pete with their eyes? He wades closer to the bed, certain now, yes; he's being watched. Circling the memory, he notices Fox has draped his weight over Ethan's back, planted his hand on Ethan's folded leg. It's a lot of touching, even by Fox's standards. Stranger still, Ethan's arms and neck have broken out in goosebumps.

Pete scrunches his brow.

The skulls erupt like a studio audience, strobing their light-up pupils, blasting their pre-recorded laughter. Pete, horrified, slings a pillow at the thick of them—*poof!*—they scatter in a scurrying pulse across the cankers and abscesses of the corroded stone walls, and gather in the darkest corner of the room, plastic carapaces clacking. Bumped from the swarm, one hits the water shell-down, a million orange tendrils flailing frantically from its plated belly. It flips itself, skates the surface like a crab... swims, cackling, between

Pete's legs. Pete yelps, thrashes, cries, "Fox!" But his cries are muted by fathoms.

Fox settles into the depths, sundering the void with sparks of stirred plankton and the beam of Pete's LED, mapping by segments an underwater corridor jeweled by tens—maybe hundreds—of thousands of memories stored in darkness, stored in fibrillating glass globes as small as barnacles, and as large as watermelons, seated in sockets upon a sculpted ceramic crag. Way off, a shimmer dances in the murk—light shining from some opening above—promising passage to further reaches of the cavern, if Fox could hold his breath long enough to swim there. He's pretty sure he can't, even with a refill. Speaking of, he's due one now. But wait, what's—

A cloud of radiation blossoms beyond the shimmer. And then there's a burst of incandescence, damn near nuclear, that throws stretching shadows along the fibrillating walls, and a beast (is it indeed a shark?) blasts out of the darkness, obscured by a boiling envelope of light, whisking the waters into a blazing inferno.

Fox gapes to scream, spews simmering light and just barely dodges the rocket, dropping Pete's keys into the reef below as he thrashes desperately for the surface.

"Help!" he croaks, breaching, feet kicking, inflaming the plankton. Irresistible bait.

He prepares himself for a grisly demise, and then feels one of Pete's strong hands grasp firmly 'round his left wrist, and the other under his armpit, and he's yanked right up out of the light.

"I told you!" Pete yells, ferocious.

"Shit," Fox says, gasping. "That was close." He chuckles nervously, massages his armpit. Sharp pain. Like something might have torn. Also, what changed? Fox's eyes flick to the congregation of skulls, clustered, clattering in the corner.

"Let me have my keys."

"Shit, dude, I dropped 'em."

"Stop joking, man. I'm going back. I'm so done with this place."

"I'm not joking this time, I swear."

"You... are the fucking worst."

"I know, I'm sorry. I'll get 'em back."

"How?"

"I dunno."

"God, you're such a dumbass." Pete says, and shakes his head, breaks the slightest grin. Fox takes that to mean he won't be holding a grudge. That's such an unbelievable relief, because if Fox didn't have Pete, well, it's just better not to even imagine.

Took them some time to feel their way out of those lower chambers without Pete's LED, Fox leading the way by the prickling of his strange new senses, Pete insisting they missed their turnoff, but the boys pour forth presently from the earth, into the golden light of a dwindling day.

Back in Reality Land, the downpour has let up to a sparse patter that barely breaks through the canopy, even if a distant rumbling thunder promises more. Birds and insects chirp and chatter, enjoying the recess. The rain-bolstered creek gushes and gurgles downstream. From a neighborhood street nearby, comes the occasional slurping swish of car tires skating across wet pavement. Everything seems just so... flat. Rendered in fewer dimensions, by fewer senses.

Pete stumbles, rickety. Fox examines his hands, as if surprised to find them solid. A mild updraft might float him, if not for the sopping weights strapped to his feet, the sepulchral rags once again smothering his body. Ethan's funeral service, which, below, had begun to feel a lifetime away, now seems as fresh and weighty to Fox as it had not two hours before.

Pete kneels at the freshwater surge, retches, but nothing comes. "Fuck," he finally says, then spits, wipes his chin and slumps back onto his ass.

"You okay?" Fox takes a seat in the mud beside him, sympathizing deeply with his struggle to reacclimate.

"So we're just accepting this as reality now?"

"What else can we do?"

"Seal it up."

"That's not funny."

"It's not a joke. I kinda mean it."

"Why?"

"Serious? Fox? It feels fucking weird in there, man. Bad. Like, wrong, super fucking wrong."

"Wrong how?"

Pete turns, studies him. "Do you really not feel it?"

Fox shrugs.

"It's like... the worst depression, times a million. It's fucking oppressive. And it just gets worse the deeper you go, gets all inside you." His fingers rake the mud as if to scratch an Earth-itch. "You think that's how he felt?"

Fox hunches over his knees, hugs his shins. He can only hope not. But then, who knows. "Maybe it doesn't feel bad 'cause of Ethan. Maybe it just feels bad 'cause of the funeral and everything, like maybe we brought that."

"Maybe." Pete doesn't buy it, and neither does Fox.

A couple of minutes pass, both boys silently reflecting on the experience of the cave, the memories of which grow murkier each passing moment. Like a dream, its detail is hard to hold onto. Everything not cemented by immediate recall simply fades.

"You going back to school?"

"Dunno. I may just go back after break."

"What about finals?"

"I don't give a shit."

Pete sorta grunts. Fox can't read it.

"I guess you're going back?"

"I have to."

"No, you don't."

"I'm not gonna fail my finals."

"Who cares?"

"What if you have to repeat?"

"Fuck that. I'll just drop out."

"Fox."

"What? There's way more important things than school."

"Yeah, well, that's easy to say, when—"

"What?"

Pete finds a rock, skips it. "He's in three of my classes. I just keep picturing his empty desks."

Fox's eyes crank shut. For him, it's the lunchroom, where he'll dine alone from now on, unless Pete returns to him, which Fox really doubts, or else invites him to join with the lacrosse guys. *No, thank you.*

"Do you think we should tell his family... "

Fox's eyes bug out. "No," he says, almost pleading,

horrified by the thought of anyone else intruding into that sacred dimension, even if, truth be told, they have more right to it than he does.

"Okay, but someone's gonna hear him." He means the uprooted Graham Enders, who's still over there playing peek-a-boo with no one in particular.

"No, they won't."

Pete flashes his eyes: *okay then*. "I think I'm gonna go."

"Can we leave your ladder?"

"Whatever, I guess. No one uses it."

"You wanna meet here tomorrow?"

Pete rakes for another rock, finds a big one and flings it way upstream. *Thunk.* "I'unno, man."

"Don't you wanna see what all's down there?"

"What do you think we're gonna find?"

Fox shrugs, brow heavy.

"I think maybe you were right. Maybe there's some things in there I don't need to know."

"Like what?" Fox asks, panicking a little internally. *Does he know? Is he mad? Does he hate me?*

"I don't know. It's not really my business, is it?"

Oh, shit. He definitely knows.

Pete rises, brushes mud off the seat of his jeans. "Are you going back in?"

"Prob'ly."

"I really don't think you should go in there alone."

"Well, what am I supposed to do if you won't go with me?"

"If I come back tomorrow, will you promise just to go home?"

"K," Fox says, not fully certain he means it.

"K..." Pete lingers, watching as some kind of torment makes waves of Fox's countenance.

"Is it—" Fox cuts himself off. He knows he shouldn't ask. No, definitely not, but he can't help himself. "My fault?"

"No, god damn it, stop saying that." Pete offers his hand. "S'go."

"You go ahead."

Pete sighs.

"I'm not going back in, I promise. I just need to sit here."

"Come sit at my house."

"You go sit at your house. I'm cool here."

"Bro."

"Get!" Fox cups the stream, whips it up at Pete. "Go on, git!" he shouts, hillbilly as can be.

"Alright," Pete says, laughing, "I'm going."

And so he does.

"Peek-a-boo!"

Know what, Amigo?

Fox drops into the crater, packs the guy's mouth with mud, breaks the newly formed roots, and dumps him through the Sphincter of Madness, winces as the old man ricochets off the aluminum ladder—*clank!*—and piles head-first into a twisted heap. *Yikes.*

Sights aplenty, even here on the surface. Almost overwhelming, this little garden of many wonders. So much so that Fox failed to notice before. Scattered among the vacation souvenirs are a few snow globes, like the ones below, that host personal memories. He gently plucks one from its hidey hole, leaving its fluorescent orange roots to dangle as from the stem of a weeded flower. Inside, there's a depiction of what Fox presumes must have been the first time Ethan went to Pride with his dad as a fifth grader. Fox can remember the sparkles in Ethan's eyes when he told of the experience. The two are pictorialized here—not in ceramic, but as tiny flesh figures—with painted faces, waving rainbow flags, Graham in a *Proud Dad* T-shirt. Precious memory. Fox pets the globe tenderly, combs back its roots... and slips it into his jacket pocket.

Better not to chance any passers-by, he climbs back up and works a while, snapping saplings and piling them over the dig.

SIX
INTEGRATION

"Where have you been?" That's concern, not malice. Fox is in the garage, shedding his wet suit. Mom just walked in on him.

"Went for a walk."

"In the rain? You're gonna get sick."

Shrug: *couldn't care less.*

"Hungry?"

Shrug: *could eat.*

Luckily, she's gotten pretty good at deciphering the hidden meanings in his disaffected gestures. I guess you do when the bulk of your ongoing communication is reduced to them. "Sandwich? Pizza rolls? I could go out and get something."

"I'll just make a sandwich."

"I'll make it. Turkey?" she asks with an expectant grin.

"Hey, don't call me Turkey." It's an old joke he just can't bring himself to adorn with any mock defensiveness—that would take too much spirit to conjure—but even unadorned, he hopes it will be enough to say, *don't worry, I'm okay.*

Of course, the rote recital says otherwise. She churns out

a pained smile. She taps her fingers rhythmically on the doorframe. "K," she says, barely a whisper, and heads off to start on the sandwich.

"Mom?"

She returns.

"I'm not gonna do what he did."

His directness catches her fully off guard. "No, I know."

"You don't have to worry about me."

"I know, but I do." She dawdles, clearly deliberating: to speak, or not to speak... "You were so brave."

Fox's eyes clamp shut and his face knots up.

"At the creek. What you did, tried to do."

Stop. Mom, please. Just stop.

"I'm so proud."

How can you be proud? I fucking failed him.

"Your dad would be so proud."

His face roils. Emotions raging to be known. He fights to bottle them.

"I've just been wanting to say that."

He holds it together until she goes inside. The very moment the door shuts behind her, he collapses atop the cold concrete, a sobbing wreck.

Slung over the shower rod, Fox's funeral garb drips into the upstairs bathtub. His snowy keepsake, pulsating with the rhythm of a human heart, graces his bed. Fox himself is downstairs, putting in his requisite Mom Time.

The sandwich was okay. Its plated remains rest atop the coffee table. Some spiky-haired tool is showing houses to newlyweds on TV. Mom's over there snoring. Fox has his phone out, ears plugged. He's researching the phenomenon, Googling every word combination he thinks could possibly describe it: trip caverns, psychic reverb, memory fungus, death caves. That last one turns up a pretty cool indie band. Fox drops a few tracks into a playlist entitled NEUSHIT. So, *cool*, that's a win, but if whatever's happening now has ever happened before, he can't find any mention of it.

Couple hours later, Fox is showering and auditioning Pete in a few jerk-off fantasies. Few times he's tried to redirect his thoughts to Ethan, but that boy arrives each time cold and milky-eyed. Needless to say, that's a boner-wilter. In the end, it's Summer who does the trick. Go figure.

Fox resists the urge to escape into the Psychic Brine songs. He's afraid of killing them. He tends to do that when he falls in love with something new. He'll grab hold with both hands, squeeze and twist, until all the magic's wrung out of a thing. It was fear that forced restraint with Ethan. If he wants to delay the inevitable with these tunes, then Death Caves will have to play him off tonight. But before the curtains close, goodnight to his tiny friends. He takes up his plucked snow globe, spins it between his fingertips. Surprisingly, it's the old man and not Ethan that captivates him. So full of life and love. So happy. You wouldn't know him from the man at the funeral. *God, he looked so... ruined.* This Graham doesn't know yet, his world will end.

The globe pulses only weakly now, never swelling

enough to erase the pleats at its poles. Its roots seem paler, almost translucent; its water, murkier, slightly yellowed. *Hope it's not sick.* He'll have to remember to plant it tomorrow. Take one of the empty pots and some soil from the back patio. Water it too. Yeah, that should probably do.

Nighty night, sleep tight, don't let death bite.

Onto his belly, eyes shut, and into the void, body sloshed by invisible waves, echoes of the cavern's persistent sense of motion. Drifting, he returns there, explores the chambers in memory, at least the parts he can still remember. The basic architecture's there, but much of the detail eludes him. Still, he makes it down to that deepest point, imagines what lies beyond the guarded waterway, what secrets possibly remain.

A teardrop tickles the ramp of his nose.

Pete creeps down the carpeted stairs and out the front door. Technically, he has no curfew, but he knows his parents wouldn't be too pleased to find him sneaking out at almost two in the morning to jump into a yellow Mini Cooper piloted by a tipsy blonde (even if her overalls and Coke bottle glasses suggest an endearing harmlessness). He gropes for his keys: missing. *Goddamnit, Fox.*

"Hiii," Summer slurs, and opens up for a hug as Pete swings into the passenger seat.

"Hey." He slugs the rearview. "Shit, sorry."

"Are you drunk?" she accuses playfully.

"No." He chuckles. "Are you?"

"Not at all." She angles the mirror back into place with a

hand covered in ink. Not tattoos, but notes and doodles. She's always writing all over her hands. "You smell good."

"Really?" He sniffs his clothes, skin, but his olfaction's warped. Like Fox, he's brought something back with him. The scent of blood. Burrowed into his nostrils. Polluted his dinner so terribly, he had to go without. Thank God that's not what Summer's getting off him.

"Where you wanna go?"

Pete stuffs his hands into his hoodie pouch and plunges them into his lap; his dick's getting a little worked up over the way she's fidgeting with the shift knob. "Wherever."

"Should we get ice cream?"

As it turns out, everything's closed, so twenty minutes later they're at her house. The kitchen, specifically. Pete's in the shadows, drumming his thighs, watching her collect two spoons and a pint of Blue Bell Cookies 'n Cream.

"Summer?" That's Mom, calling from wherever the master bedroom is. Somewhere close by the sound of it. Pete's been over a couple times before, but he never got a tour or anything, so the layout's a mystery. Especially in the dark. At least he doesn't have to worry about any sharks.

"Yeah, I'm home. Goodnight." She grins, puts a finger to her lips, then takes his hand, guides him upstairs.

He feels aflutter to think the condom he's carried in his velcro wallet since seventh grade (so long, it's sculpted a permanent ring-shaped bulge into the coin pouch), might finally see some action, if it hasn't disintegrated.

For a brief moment, it feels like he's starting to flow

again, off and to the right, as in the cave. He slows, grips the banister, wags his head to shake it off.

"Okay?" she asks, towering over him from one step up.

He nods.

And suddenly, Summer's some kind of witch, casting happy spells through a magic smile.

She tugs his hand and on they go.

Hers is the only room on the third floor. Sunflowers, stuffed animals, absurdly large bed, canopy of gauzy fabrics and white string lights. She puts on some dreamy music, takes off her sweater, kicks off her shoes and flops onto the pillowy platform.

Pete checks out a painting-in-progress on an expensive easel: portrait of a giraffe-necked, Picasso-faced girl that might be Summer herself, outlined in concentric bands of trite poetry. Pete cringes. Although he owns a couple of pieces, her art's so totally not his thing. Especially not now that she got onto this kick, scribbling words over everything. Words on art, just the worst. So tryhard, unlike Fox's work, which lacks any pretension, ambition, or self-consciousness. Pete chastises himself for thinking such unkind thoughts about such a kind girl. *Cool colors, at least*, he thinks, wanting to give it some credit. *God, I'm an asshole.* "Is this you?" he asks.

Summer blushes. "Just a girl."

"Looks like you."

Summer offers a spoon to Pete. He joins her on the bed. She pops the lid on the pint, stabs the ice cream. Too frozen to penetrate. "Needs to melt."

Their eyes lock. Unbearable intensity. Pete drops onto his back, stares up at the canopy of twinkling lights.

"How are you?" she asks.

"Okay. How are you?"

"I mean with everything. Are you okay? I was really worried when you didn't call."

"Yeah, I know. Sorry. I've just had the most fucked up day."

"You look tired."

He drapes an arm across his face. "Can't really sleep."

"How was the funeral?"

"Okay, I guess. I spoke."

"What'd you say?"

"Just some shit. I dunno."

"You don't wanna say?"

He sighs.

"You don't have to."

"I was just rambling. I dunno. I said how he was always like this mystery, even from when I first met him. You never knew what he was thinking, but you could always tell whatever it was might change the world." He snorts, embarrassed by the sincerity. "I dunno, I said how he was always watching nature documentaries on YouTube and telling me the most interesting parts, and how he told me once about this video he'd seen about this mushroom, just regular brown from the outside, but when you cut it open, its insides would blush this rainbow of colors. I said Ethan was like that, when you got him to open up. He didn't laugh that often, but when he did, he'd burst so loud, it'd almost startle you, and you'd feel so proud having earned that. I said that was my favorite thing about him, when you could get him to laugh really big that way. I said I hope wherever he is now, there'll be someone to make him laugh."

"I wish I knew him better," Summer says, sniffles.

"Yeah."

"Kinda wish I came today."

He's actually kinda glad she didn't. Better she's sort of an escape from all that. It's not like they were actually friends or anything anyway, she and Ethan, outside of her connection through him. Or through Fox. Technically she and Fox were friends—or friendly—from art class before Pete met her.

"How's Fox?"

"Fucked up I think." Pete chuckles nervously.

"Aw. They were really close."

"Yeah, I guess." He peels his arm away, meets her warm gaze. "I keep having these dreams where... " He stops himself. Maybe that's telling too much.

"Yeah?"

"I find him out there, like we did Ethan." His voice quivers.

"He wouldn't though, right?"

"I don't think so, but I never thought Ethan would either."

"You didn't have any idea?"

"No, I mean." He groans, sits up."Fuck, I dunno."

"What?"

He shakes his head.

"We don't have to talk about it."

"I almost didn't go either."

"Why?"

"Scared, I guess. To see Fox. I hadn't seen him since—" Pete pauses, twitches. "He thinks it's his fault, but it's mine." Pete almost, *almost* loses it.

"How?"

"I left him, right there where he did it."

Summer moves the spoons and ice cream to the night table, scoots closer. "It's not anyone's fault."

He watches, enraptured, as her lips stretch toward her ears. The resulting smile broadcasts July fireworks, night swims, bare feet on hot pavement, everything good and right in this world. He closes his eyes, slips fingers between the snaps of his shirt, rubs his cool chest, bathing, *thawing* in her glow. Then her cushiony lips press against his, and suddenly he's adrift in a sea of vanilla-gloss-flavored Summer waves, into which the rest of the world melts, dissolves...

He'd gladly float there forever, but the waves recede, beaching him on the shore of his own desert island. He opens his eyes and the world reconstitutes. Summer's only inches away, but the distance feels insurmountable.

"Thank you," he whispers.

"You're welcome," she says, and blushes.

SEVEN
PSYCHONAUTS

The morning's warming up nicely; birds and insects rejoice. Remnants of the ceaseless overnight showers bejewel the trees, sunder golden sunbeams into spectral fans. Beautiful day for a psychedelic spelunking expedition. Fox woke Pete early with a text: *meet at the creek?* Pete rose reluctantly, put on old clothes, but the culvert is as far as he's willing to go on his own.

Fox skates the concrete slope on a pile of leaves, suited for the adventure in backpack, boardshorts, and his neon windbreaker (the one that means trouble). "You ready, boy?" He brandishes a broomstick with a kitchen knife duct-taped to the tip.

Pete eyeballs the homemade spear, lip curling to imagine. "What's that for?"

"Fishing." Fox tries his devil's smirk.

"Great."

"You feel any better?"

"Sure. You?"

"I feel okay."

"That's good."

"Totally." Fox stabs the mud, cranks his arm back, snags a disposable water bottle from his backpack's side holster, takes a swig of its swampy contents, chokes. "Try this."

"What's in it?"

"Little a'this, little a', oh, *everything*."

"You made a suicide?"

That takes Fox a second. "Shit. I didn't even think of that." But now that he has, it eats him alive. "I just thought, so we wouldn't get caught."

"Give it here," Pete says, interrupting Fox's pity party. Fox forks over the bottle and Pete samples his handiwork... "Jesus."

"Good, huh?"

"Surprised it didn't melt the bottle."

Fox goes off giggling. "Prob'ly make napalm if we put it in styrofoam."

"No kidding." Fox's breath, and his swaying posture: dead giveaways. Pete realizes Buddy Boy's stolen more than a little head start on him. Which, yeah. *Bit concerning*, eight o'clock Sunday morning. Pete returns the bottle. "Thought you were gonna bring orange juice."

"Didn't have any." Fox holsters the suicide. "I brought some snacks and shit, though."

"Let's not stay down there too long, though, okay?"

"K."

"We just look around a little bit and then we come back up. And if we feel alright after that, I don't know, maybe we go back down again, okay?"

"Yeah, whatever."

"You act like this is all nothing."

Fox shrugs, claims his spear from the ground.

"It's fucking weird, man. And it's scary to me, you don't seem to get that."

"Don't be scared. I'll protect you."

"That's not what I meant."

Nonetheless, down the sphincter Fox goes.

Pete, God help him, follows, into Ethan's bedroom, through the Trial of Sanity, so dubbed, down the two-way telescoping bluff of the waterfall, to the shelf of carpeted star-boulders that rim the grotto, where their presence draws the color-changing shark to the surface, its fin cutting the floating pages of pornography.

"Aw, someone's 'cited to see you."

"Oh my god, Fox, you're so funny."

Fox pouts his lip, mimicking young Ethan. "It's still God's creature."

"You sure about that?"

"What, you didn't realize Ethan was God?"

"Who's that, then, Jesus?"

That really sends Fox off on a fit of laughter.

"What's that thing have to do with Ethan, anyway?

"I dunno, but it does somehow." Fox prostrates himself before the lip of the lagoon, primes his spear, and rakes his free fingers through the brine. "Here fishy," he calls, as if to a pet.

"I hope you get bit," Pete says, and steps over him, makes his way across the crescent ledge toward the beach.

"Mr. Fishy, Mr. Fishy."

The shark dives, uninterested in the bait.

"Throw that napalm over here."

Fox draws the bottle from his bag, pitches it across the grotto; it lands several feet short, thuds into the damp polychrome sand of the shore, where it's immediately lapped by a wave and drawn bobbing into the shallows.

Pete flings his hands up: *are you kidding?* "You can't throw for shit."

"You could have caught that."

Pete borrows Mr. Enders's pool skimmer.

Fox lowers himself onto his belly, swipes a window through the porn.

"Rawr!" The shark lunges, blasts Fox with its sulphurous breath as its razor chompers clack shut, just missing Fox's arm.

Fox tumbles, screaming, flailing with his spear; he jabs it through the surface, grazes neon flesh. Blood puffs. The beast jets.

"I cut it!"

"Leave it alone."

"Nah, I'm gonna kill it so we can swim."

"I thought you wanted to explore."

"We have all day."

"I'm not staying in here all day. And I'm not getting in any water."

"Even if I kill it?"

"Why you wanna hurt it anyway, if this is all Ethan? Just leave it be, man."

That cuts like a buzz saw, the way only truth can. Pete's right. That's fucked, so totally fucked to kill it, even if it did try to kill them. Fox watches with regret as the red swirls dissipate. *Poor thing.* He hauls himself up and crosses the ledge to the beach.

"It's weird," Pete says. "This morning I could barely remember anything from inside here. Like, I couldn't even picture it at all. The whole thing felt like a dream."

"I think it is like a dream. You have to make a point to remember as soon as you go up, like to convert it into a lower dimension while you're still coming down." Fox stabs his blade into the sand, slings his backpack across his shoulder and digs out a battery-powered camping lantern, offers it to Pete. "Here, you carry this. I got the spear."

Pete holsters the suicide in Fox's side pouch, takes the lamp.

"I brought goggles too, just in case," Fox says and absolutely loses it, laughing at Pete's comical glare.

"Guess what. I hung out with Summer last night."

"Rad. You still going back to school tomorrow?"

"Yeah, you?"

"So, what, y'all're dating now or something?"

"Are you mad?"

"No. I'm just asking."

"I dunno. We kissed."

"Ohmygod, tell me everything."

"Don't be mad."

"I'm not."

"I thought you'd be happy."

Fox snorts. "Happy?"

"I mean, whatever. It was Ethan's idea."

"How?"

"He's the one who said I should ask her out." Pete approaches the entry to the locker room. "This is the one you went in before?"

"Yeah, but it's just, like, people making fun of Ethan and shit. Let's go a different way."

Pete steps beyond the threshold, shines the light into the space.

"Pete, please."

"What?" Pete asks, bewildered.

"Just please don't. I don't want you to see."

Something in Fox's expression, some apparent desperation, convinces Pete to relent. "Okay," he says and steps away. "You lead."

Back through the hidden alcove off the beach, along the trickling runnel, down the shallow steps of that gentle helix, to the left this time at the fork, the path routes them deeper, deeper into that throbbing murk, that invasive malaise, into—

An elementary school classroom, grown askew, geography misaligned with that of the chamber, so that the cross-legged students span the wall to the partially-carpeted pits and bulges of the ceiling, where several hang upside down like bats, pupils reflecting the light of Pete's lantern. The teacher, sprouted out of the craggy carpeted wall along with her chair at a pitch of some thirty degrees, reads from *The Lion, The Witch And The Wardrobe*. Several students screech suddenly and scatter from a very young Ethan perched up where the tableau turns over itself. A dark spot radiates through his jeans and urine dribbles down the carpeted wall in highlighter-yellow rivulets that adhere to the cave's gravity, as opposed to that of the memory. "I told you I couldn't hold it," he says, and cries.

"It feels wrong to be seeing this," Pete says, sympathetically miserable.

"Why?"

"What if someone went crawling all through your most embarrassing memories?"

"I wouldn't mind."

"Right."

"If it was you or Ethan, I wouldn't."

"Then what are you trying to hide?"

"I'm not hiding anything."

Pete flashes his eyes.

"That's different."

"How?"

"Because I'm still alive." Regret tangles Fox's features, even before he's through speaking.

"Nice."

"What if he wants us to see?"

"You really believe that?"

"Maybe he's trying to show us something."

"Like what?"

"I dunno." Fox whimpers. "Why he fucking did this."

Pete glances around. Have they stumbled into a dead end? "Which way?" he asks very softly, by way of consolation. If it helps Fox to explore, fine, they'll explore, but it seems certain they'll have to turn back.

"You feel that?"

"What?"

Fox gestures to his legs. A low-hanging jetstream whips his shin hairs.

Pete watches—honestly a little unsettled by his buddy's evident sixth sense for this place—as Fox traces the current to a tunnel bored into the painted-cinder-block rock face, its opening barely wide enough, if even, to wedge a body through. But Fox, undaunted, chucks his backpack and spear ahead, and, before Pete can object, launches himself, skull-print sneakers kicking behind.

"You're gonna get stuck."

"Nuh-uh," Fox's muffled sing-song retort returns, and sure enough not. "Let me have the light."

Pete passes the lantern through the opening, and the shadows rush to gobble him. He fumbles for his keyring, eyes bursting with fireworks, and, finding them missing (oh yeah), curses once more Fox's recklessness. "What's in there?"

"It's safe. There's no water. Come on."

Pete never considered himself claustrophobic, but the thought of cramming himself through that tiny passage has him breaking out in a cold sweat. If he corks the hole, then Fox is trapped, and they're both screwed. "Let's go another way."

"What other way?"

"I won't fit."

"Yes, you will. Come on."

Goddamnit. Pete drops to his knees, then to his belly, and starts squirming. Halfway through, he gets caught. *Oh shit. Okay, okay. Back up.* He tries, but he's too thoroughly wedged, only succeeds in bunching the tail of his shirt uncomfortably under his ribs. *Shit, Shit! I can't breathe!* "I'm stuck!"

"No, you're not, just wiggle."

"I *am* wiggling!"

"Try going back."

"I can't!"

"Well, just wait here, then, I'll go see if I can find some K-Y." Fox makes to head off with the light.

"That's not funny. Fox, that's not funny! Please!"

"Are you really stuck?"

"Yes!" Pete cries, rock formations jabbing his hips, ribs, shoulders.

"Well, don't freak out." Fox sets the lamp down. "You'll make it worse."

"It's not a goddamn finger trap."

Fox cackles.

"It's not funny," Pete repeats, almost pleads.

"Oh, I see the problem."

"What?"

"It's them birthin' hips."

"I don't have birthin' hips, asshole, just pull me."

Fox reaches in, all Stretch Armstrong, takes Pete's hand and tugs.

"Wait, wait, stop. That hurts. Let go, stop, that fucking hurts."

Fox releases him. "Dude. Just wiggle."

He gets his body squirming and doesn't let up until he finds an angle that frees him, and then bursts through like a fired cannonball. He picks himself up, examines the stinging scrapes on his arms and elbows. "I hate this place."

"Don't say that." Fox says and looks around, as if worried the cave might overhear.

"I fucking do."

Fox hands him the lantern. By its light, Pete sees they've entered a vaulted chamber, walls piled in overlapping drips and rivulets, as if the plaster once ran fluid. It's Ethan's parents' bedroom, or so Pete supposes, because a decade-fresher Graham plays human rolling pin, up and down the length of the king-size bed while a tiny Ethan (four, five years old?) and Ellie (eight?) giggle and bound over him, doing their best to avoid being flattened. "You're not gonna get me, Roly Poly!" Ethan squeals.

The whole scene's cobwebbed, as if long forgotten, dusted in blankets of settled ash that the boys' invasion stirs into the atmosphere. Pete masks his face with his shirt neck, wonders if the blight must signify something. Some illness—depression, maybe—accreting until any trace of light or joy is snuffed out. God only knows what it's doing to their lungs. Pete checks Fox, sees that he's lost in thought, maybe aching for his own dad. Never did there live a boy who admired his father more. "Hop up."

Fox throws down his weapon and leaps onto the bed with the kids, each bounce drawing thick plumes of charcoal from the mattress.

"You won't get me, Roly Poly," Ethan cries, again.

"Yeah, you won't get us, Roly Poly!" No sooner does Fox proclaim as much than his foot is captured, and he falls yelping under the steamroller.

"Look what you did, dumbass."

Fox resurrects himself from playing dead, sees that his antics have derailed the entire memory, sent Pops ramping off the bed, wiping out the siblings on his way. "Oops." He jumps down, dusts himself off. "Should I set them back up, you think?"

"What for?" Pete moves along with the lantern.

Fox reclaims his blade and follows—

Into a reproduction of the woods from the surface above, or an enclosed portion anyway. The replica's a little confused, the boys find, stepping through the charcoal-loaded trees: blue faux fur for foliage on some of the branches; fiber optic filaments fanning like light-up pine needles on others; that orange-beaded soft drink oozing like pitch from knotholes; everything dimly starlit, meaning bathed in the eerie green glow coming off countless crawling plastic paste-ons overhead.

Fox hangs his weight off a flexible branch, then lets

spring a great billowing eruption of ash that sheds all over the boys and the scenery.

Pete manages to suppress an oncoming sneeze, but not the second, third, or any other in what becomes a chain of six, each more violent than the last.

"Bless you," Fox says, amused.

"Thanks, dude. Was just thinking how great it'd be if we got sick from being in here." Pete presses on, into a clearing, into... their smokespot, where clones of Fox and Ethan are huddled by the stream; Fox, fourteen years old; Ethan, barely fifteen; both wearing suits, Fox lying on his shoulder in the blackened mud, head resting in Ethan's lap, Ethan petting his hair while Fox burns a leaf with his Bic.

Pete looks back at his companion, who grabs a tree to keep from collapsing.

"When was this?"

Barely a whisper, barely audible: "After the funeral."

"Your dad?"

Fox lifts his chin: an anemic nod.

"Where was I?"

"Don't remember," Fox says coldly, and breaks away.

He does remember, though. And clearly. They'd come out after the service, the three of them. Fox can remember Ethan and Pete trying to lift his spirits with the occasional joke, but mostly they just sat together, drank a bottle of booze Fox had pilfered from home. Night rolled around and Pete left to go work on a history project. Fox didn't want to go home, so Ethan stayed with him a while longer. Fox can remember trying to wrap his head around the idea that his dad was history, that all their experiences together were history. He can remember thinking that Pete should do his project on Dad, because *who could give a shit about Christopher*

Columbus or any of those assholes, whose contributions to yesteryears would never mean half as much as those made by his dad in terms of shaping his world. He can remember laying his head in Ethan's lap shortly thereafter, free then to be truly vulnerable. He can remember how wonderful and reassuring those fingers felt in his hair, how much love they radiated, reminding him that although the brightest light in all the world had gone out, he hadn't been left in total darkness.

So, yeah, good question: *where were you?* Barely knew Ethan then, or, that's not really fair, but they'd only known each other a short time in the scheme of things, yet there he was when Fox needed him. *Where were you?*

Pete follows Fox to where the creek ought to be. Instead, there's a chasm. Pete shines the lantern into the endless depths. The younger Fox tosses a burning leaf into the crevasse. It twirls and twirls... until it's reduced to a glittering pinpoint... and then vanishes.

"Who pulled out the plug?"

Fox doesn't laugh, nor even grin.

Pete's own smile recedes.

Fox toes a stone over the edge, counts off an incredible thirteen Mississippi before the echoes of its splashy collision return. *I should look up how real cavers do it. Maybe add rope and shit to my Christmas list.*

"I know what you're hiding."

Fox studies Pete. Does he? Fox shrugs: *so?*

"Why won't you just say it?"

"Why should I if you already know?"

They stand off, each testing the other with a scrutinizing glare. "I'm done, man," Pete finally says, breaking the silence and the eye contact.

"Go, then."

"I don't wanna leave you."

"Why not?"

"Because."

"Just go. I don't care. It's just been me and Ethan all year anyway, so it's not like this is anything different."

"Dude."

"What?"

"Why are you trying to be an asshole?"

"I'm not trying to be anything. If you think I'm an asshole, I guess I am."

"Stop."

"Just fucking go. Go back to school. Go fuck Summer. I *don't* care."

Pete nods. "I'm taking the fucking lamp." And he does.

"I hope you get stuck!" Good one, robbed of its zing by too long a delay, but it didn't occur to Fox immediately.

Abandoned in the almost romantic pale glow of the fiber optic trees, and the crawling stars, Fox drops down on hand and knees, screams Ethan's name into the crevasse. Thirteen seconds later, his own voice returns to him, multiplied into a chorus of ghostly reflections. Not echoes exactly, he realizes, distinguishing a whisper and a squeaky voice crack from the rest, but randomly culled memories—playback of many different times in the past when he's called Ethan's name, all layered up into a horrible scalp-tingling cacophony. He folds his arms over his head and curses himself for chasing off the only friend he has left.

Fox races back to the grotto, hoping to head Pete off at the beach, stop him from leaving by whatever means necessary, even by apology, should it come to that. But Pete hasn't left. Fox can see the lamp's glow moving through the otherwise lightless locker room. Fox stabs the sand with his spear, shrugs off his backpack, and heads in to own up to it.

"Keep your eyes to your fucking self in the locker room," Cam hisses, spattering young Ethan with spittle.

Fox leans against the cool lockers, watches Pete, who regards the scene stone-faced, without comment. "Pete," Fox says finally, tortured by the silence.

"Why didn't you do something?" He no doubt would have.

"I'm sorry."

"Is this okay?" It's quiet, yeah—Ethan's voice—but Pete hears it, and continues on.

"Pete, please."

He doesn't relent. Not this time. He tracks the voice (and the scent of petrichor) through the showers...

Fox waits. This, he can't watch. He crumples onto the concrete floor, hugs his knees, gets himself rocking, tugging at the loops of his shoelaces. God, he feels so fucking stupid in this ridiculous windbreaker. He rips it off.

It's a while before Pete returns, brow all bunched. Is that confusion? Disgust? Anger? He dredges his throat, spits up a wad of phlegm. "I dunno how you can stand it in here, man." He steps up to Fox, offers the lamp.

Fox looks up, eyes twinkling. Is this a peace offering? He accepts it.

Pete leaves him sitting alone.

The daylight strikes like needles against Fox's super-dilated eyes. He left his backpack, lantern, everything below, so he's got both hands with which to shade his face. Squinting, he finds Pete sitting by the shimmering stream. Fox hugs a tree and watches. Pete twists his neck a quarter-turn—the subtlest acknowledgement of Fox's presence—then gives Fox the back of his head.

"Do you honestly not feel how profoundly fucked it is in there? There's something seriously wrong with that place. It's fucking all inside me. I can taste it in my throat." He dredges up another wad of phlegm.

Fox hangs his head. Seconds pass for minutes.

"So, what, you were, like, boyfriends?"

"I dunno." Fox whimpers, frustrated. If only he could see what Pete's face is doing. He grinds his toe into the earth. "It was just a gradual thing. Like, it wasn't even romantic or sexual or anything at all, at first. I just needed him. And... I dunno what we were. We only held hands. We never even kissed. I mean, I wanted to, but I was scared."

Pete rakes the mud for a suitable skipping stone.

"You mad?"

"Why should I be mad?"

"Because. I dunno."

Pete flings his catch with enough force to skip it fully across the creek, where it cracks against a rockpile on the opposite bank. "It's just weird. I didn't even know you were gay."

"I'm not. I mean, yeah, I guess I maybe must be, or, I

dunno, bi or something, but I never felt that way about anyone else. Just him."

"This whole time?"

"I guess I always sorta thought he was... beautiful." Fox's cheeks flush brilliantly. "God, it's so weird talking to you about this. I wanted to tell you so many times."

"So, why didn't you?"

"I was embarrassed," Fox says, just absolutely agonized.

"Why?"

"I dunno. I don't mean to be embarrassed by him." Tears streak his cheeks, glitter in the golden light of the yet low-hanging sun. Fox pulls his shirt neck up to dry them.

Pete cranks his head another quarter turn, pins Fox in the corner of his eye. "I just dunno why you'd think you'd have to hide something like this from me. Like, what kinda person do you think I am that I wouldn't just be happy for you?"

"You don't seem very happy."

"Yeah, well, you try finding out you've been deceived all this time, that your two best friends would have rather been alone."

"That's not true. I always want you around."

"You should have just told me."

"How would I know how you were gonna react? You're totally different now."

"That's bullshit."

"You are."

"I'm the same as I ever was, dude. You just see me different, and it's bullshit."

"Are you coming back down?"

"I dunno what you think you're gonna find in there." Finally, he turns fully over his shoulder, makes penetrative eye contact. "Seriously, what exactly are you looking for?"

"Why he did this."

"There was something wrong with him. You feel that in there, don't you? No one does this kind of thing for just some reason. Not because he got picked on. Not because you didn't defend him, or because you were embarrassed by him. Not because of some stupid joke you made the night he died. Even the happy memories in there are covered in that black shit. There was something really, *seriously* wrong with him. I don't know why you need it to be your fault."

"Because he needed me."

"Yeah, and you did everything you could."

Fox's face knots up. He shakes his head. *It wasn't enough.*

"I know, *I know* how you feel."

"It's not the same."

"Why?"

"Because *I* loved him."

"Fuck you, man. You don't get to own him."

Fuck you, asshole. You don't have any idea what it's like.

Pete rises, brushes the mud from his ass. "I'm done, okay? I can't go back down there."

"You're just gonna give up on him?"

"I'm not giving up on him, Fox, he's fucking dead. There's nothing we can do but just accept it."

"How could I accept that?"

"Besides, if anyone gave up, it was fucking him."

I wish it was you, Fox thinks, and hates himself for it. "Just go."

Pete holds his eyes, but it's too intense. Fox has to look away.

"If you keep searching for proof you're to blame, you're gonna find it. But you're not. He made his own stupid choice, and I'm sorry, but it has nothing to do with you."

"Just fuck off, okay?"

Pete's penetrating glare never leaves Fox's face, but Fox doesn't dare meet it. "All you'll find down there is what you wanna see."

"I said, *fuck off!*" Fox's wrath echoes through the trees, stirring birds to flight.

And off Pete goes. Maybe forever.

Good.

EIGHT

SLEEPOVER

ox is hiding out in his bedroom ossuary. The skeletons are really starting to get to him, and the sludgy, mournful Death Caves track he put on is no help at all. Nor is the funky smell emanating from—oh. *Is that me?*

Cursed, the song's called. Just like he must be, because everyone he loves dies, or leaves (he conjures a mental image of that asshole, Pete, and shoots both middle fingers at him). Fox has never considered himself a believer of any sort, but some part of him must believe something, since he's been praying to his dad to find Ethan wherever he might be —if there is anything besides nothing—and keep him safe, so he doesn't have to be so scared and alone, if he is. He must be.

It's getting on into the evening and starting to rain again. Fox kicked around in the cave for maybe half an hour after Pete left, reclaimed his windbreaker, killed off the last of his alcoholic concoction, then chilled on the underground beach a while, reflecting, letting the lava and the Cold Lights battle for his body temperature. But that place only amplified his anxieties, sent him tumbling into a terrible thought-spiral. Best not to trip when you're feeling that way. Set and setting, and all that. So he came home and went straight up to bed. But this place is worse. He's starting to think maybe he *should* go to school tomorrow. Just to have somewhere to be.

His mom looked in on him a bit ago, asked how he felt about giving it a try. *No,* he told her, doing his best impression of himself, sober, although she had to smell the alcohol on him. If she did, she didn't say so. Only said she'd phone the front office in the morning, see what can be done about finals.

Goodbye Death Caves, hello television. The light box, not the band. Fox flips too rapidly for any human to possibly distinguish any one channel from the next (a frequent complaint of his mom's). It's all bullshit anyway. *Click.*

To his laptop, then. He pastes the Psychic Brine links into a YouTube downloader. His big idea: dump them shits into his video editor, fiddle with the brightness and contrast, find out once and for all what's in the darkness...

But a pop-up interrupts. A message forwarded from his phone, from Pete. To even see that name sends his stomach tripping on a make-believe gravity drop.

Pete: *Summer wants to know if she can call you.*

There ought to be a GIF of Fox's expression: the perfect *the-fuck?* face. *Why,* he writes.

Pete:

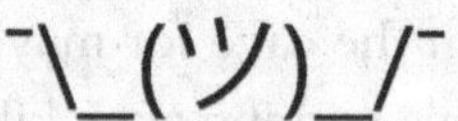

No doubt, Pete told her everything. *Fuck them.* Fox shoots back a middle finger emoji.

So weird, he knows now. Fox guesses it probably makes a certain kinda sense Pete's so triggered about being "deceived." Found out really young his dad was carrying on behind his mom's back. That's why he started speaking Spanish at home, which had always embarrassed him before, as a way to alienate his monolingual father. *Get over it, bro. 'Least you still have your dad.*

So, wait... oh yeah, the videos...

It's really impossible to overstate the disappointment Fox experiences when he finds there isn't anything in them at all.

Midnight. Mom's almost always asleep by now, but Fox stops outside her door to make sure, listens for her tell-tale honking breaths. Clear. Cool. Off to the woods, then, windbreaker and boardshorts protecting him from the drizzle, but not from the cold. He's shivering by the time he reaches the cave, tosses the saplings away and lowers himself into the earth, but it's a bit warmer underground, probably thanks to the lava, which must be winning its battle against the Cold Lights. He shakes out his dampened hair, looks around.

Nature's moving in, it seems. Moths and long-legged winter gnats swarm the tempestuous imprisoned phosphor clouds. And a startling hiss alerts Fox to another intruder. A sodden opossum cowers atop Ethan's desk, backs itself against the wall, mouth gaped, fangs displayed. Fox clucks his tongue at it. It answers with another hiss, a show of false bravado, but the poor thing trembles, terrified.

"Hungry?" Fox slings his backpack 'round his shoulder, digs for an Oreo. He tosses one onto the desk.It shatters, scatters in chunks. But the opossum remains paralyzed by fear. "Eat it."

It doesn't, so Fox gives up and carries on.

Through the Trial of Sanity (and a trial it certainly proves, to traverse tipsy), Fox arrives (very eventually) at the top of the waterfall. Mr. Fishy circles the lagoon below, tail thrashing. "Hi, fishy, wann'n Oreo?" Fox drops one into the water—*thunk!*

Okay, so careful, *careful*. More than tipsy, Fox realizes, he's actually still pretty goddamn drunk, and it prob'ly ain't the brightest idea to attempt this, but oh well, over the edge he goes. And, oh, it's so dizzying to negotiate, the way it all ripples and evolves, and moreover telescopes. *How did I get up this*, he wonders, trashed as he was when he left earlier, but he must have blacked that part out because there's nothing in his memory between lying on the beach and lying on his bed. The return's only half the journey anyway. No biggie, piggy, compared to this. Little more'n halfway down, figuring himself no more than a few feet up from the perspective at the bottom, Fox dispatches his foot to check for ground. *My, what long legs I have.* Stretchy-stretch, way deep into the fog. A boy could step right over the Atlantic with this kinda reach. But the fog musta made dinner of the ground, since his toes don't touch. He glances up to check his progress, sees his arms drawn out like melted cheese, drawn thinner by the moment, by gravity's claim upon his dangling load. He cries out in horror, feels his grip lubricated by grease, or by sweat, feels—way beyond his sight now—whatever plasticky knob to which he's clung begin to evolve. He gropes blindly for a more secure handhold, but his scouring arm buckles like an extended tape measure, pours slack across his face, and knocks him from his perch.

He slams hard against the rock shelf, sending up an explosion of fog, evacuating his lungs. He lies stunned a moment, indulging his defeat, then snaps to with a burst of vigor, stands on knees to inspect the damage. Ha! Nothing broken, that he can tell, so long as his ribs are merely bruised. He picks himself up, toes his way along that treacherously narrow ledge to the beach.

"I betchoo wann'n cookie," Fox slurs, and drops to his knees next to young Ethan, collapsing his (and Ellie's) sand castle. The ice crystals have returned, Fox sees. A beard of glittering shards slice out from the kid's cheek, touched by that cold teal luminescence. Fox glares up at the poppling bulbs. "Fugging lights! Where's'r stupid switch?" No switch, but he does spot his makeshift spear in the sand, just where he left it, next to the battery-powered lantern that he apparently left on. He grabs the spear and goes piñata-crazy on the *fugging* things. "Go out, go out! We don't want your stupid light!" He makes a chant of it, and a dance, paper-thin glass fragments raining over him.

That takes care of that, then.

He stumbles backward, almost—*almost*—plants his foot directly into one of the lava streams, tumbles over himself to save it, and goes down hard into the sand, onto his bad knee. He cries out in agony, sends a string of obscenities echoing throughout the cavern... which then return to him as whispers that tickle his scalp, wet his ear canals. He plugs them with shrugged shoulders, folds his arms over his head.

Across the lagoon, the shark breaches, snorts. Is it laughing? Fox throws the spear like a javelin, misses by a mile. The beast dives anyway, though, *so take that, you colorful bitch.*

Fox crawls back to young Ethan, uses his palm to melt the frost. The cold burns. *Fuck me*, does it burn. Even so, Fox doesn't give, not until the ice is thawed. "It's okay, you'll be warm now." He plants a kiss on the boy's cowlicked crown, then snags his backpack, plus lantern, and heads into the locker room.

"That what you wanna see?" Cam says, wagging his hideous dick at Ethan.

"Don't fugging touch him." Fox says, very meekly.

"No." But yeah, Ethan does steal a glance.

"Then why you lookin' at it?"

"I'm not."

Cam lunges, pins Ethan by the neck, bouncing his head off the tin.

"I said, don't fuh-king touch him!" Fox drops the lamp and pounces, blasts Cam across the lockers, topples him underneath Fox's own lesser weight—

Crack! Cam's skull opens against the puddle-ridden concrete floor. "Keep your eyes to your fucking self in the locker room," he repeats, despite the sickening concussion, despite the corona of blood radiating from his head.

"That's what you fucking get!"

Yeah, and know what else, while he's at it? Fox pins his own younger double with the most hate-filled eyes. He climbs off Cam, trips over his own feet and leverages the momentum to throw a brutal flying punch that utterly wilts that most loathsome coward: himself. Several kicks and a stomp make a bloody blimp of its face. Fox spits on the lumpy mess. Then, not yet satisfied justice has been done, he jams both hands into its shaggy hair, and drags it out to the beach.

He wrestles it into the shallows and sails it off to the deep. With very little body fat, the flesh mannequin sinks rapidly beneath the foamy surface, beneath the scattered pornography, its swollen face puffing blood, its eyes—Fox's own eyes—open, fearful not of death, but for Ethan's wellbeing, that it never so much as lifted a finger to preserve. It exhales, releases a torrent of bubbles; inhales, fills with water, and so sinks faster, into a red cloud of its own making. And, yeah, Mr. Fishy comes to claim it, shreds it apart in a thrashing frenzy that makes a slasher's paradise out of the lagoon, stirring waves that break deep red around Fox's legs as he vomits up a great geyser of his alcoholic suicide.

Head throbbing, he reels back to the sand and collapses atop his belly, facing away from the mayhem. He buries his face in the rainbow particles, covers his ears and scalp as best he can, and draws his knees underneath him.

Pete use-ta-be a hundred million times cooler when he was into making skate videos 'n soda bombs 'n shit, back 'fore he got so obsessed with school 'n lacrosse 'n working out. Wish we could just get high and go fuck around on our boards, maybe go skate the stairs at The Met. But that can't happen anymore. Or it could, but it won't, 'cause he doesn't never, ever wanna do a single thing fun anymore, 'less there's some point. We never use-ta ever have a point, but everything's different now. 'N it won't go back the way it was.

He unfurls to find the grotto serene once more, sedate, even, with the white noise of the waterfall and the soothing subsonic vibrations. He pushes up to a squat and dusts the grit off his face, arms, out of his leg hair. He digs into his backpack for the little travel bottle of ibuprofen he keeps in the front pouch. He pops three, works up enough spit to swallow them. He didn't pack anything to drink, unfortunately, besides the booze, but he needs something to erase this vile bile taste.

He tries the faucets in the locker room, but the tap water's so brackish, he may as well be eating table salt. Still, it's better than stomach acid, so he swishes, spits.

He catches a glimpse of his reflection in the mirror. He looks unbelievably ill, but that's beside the point, because faced with the visage, intoxicated by not just the alcohol, but the psychotropic effects of the cave, he sees not himself, but rather the avatar he pilots through Reality Land, as something separate from himself, *other than* himself. He can't keep from prodding its alien features.

"Is this okay?" That's Ethan's voice, from his boggy bedroom. Fox hears it, and follows, his guts yo-yoing. It was that very memory—of the first time Ethan held his hand—that drew Fox back to the cave tonight. *And there he is.* Polo shirt. Hair neatly combed (except for that cowlick he could never seem to defeat). Like a boy on picture day. Ethan always looked that way. *So beautiful.*

"Hi," Fox says, wiping the water from his chin.

Ethan doesn't respond. That's okay.

Fox drops his bag, kicks off his shoes and wades through the soupy blue quicksand, joins them on the bed, Ethan and his own likeness. He pries their fingers apart, then rolls his duplicate off into the mud. *Splat.* Fox is here now to play his own part.

"Is this okay?" Ethan asks.

"Yes," Fox says, interlacing their digits, and, God, it feels so good, tastes so good to Fox's tingling, salivating fingertips, to his thirsty palm. He lays his head on Ethan's shoulder. Smells just like the real thing, just exactly the way Ethan always smelled. Fox buries his nose there in the ridge of the collarbone, fills his lungs, his icy ear rubbing against Ethan's radiant face. He comes up, plants a kiss on that lovely warm surface. "I'm sorry," he wheezes, tears beginning to flow, wetting Ethan's cheek. Fox gently butts their heads together, nuzzles his nose back and forth. "I'm so sorry," he says, and plants another kiss, tasting his own tears. "I need you, I do." His nuzzling nose carries him off to the ear, which receives its own peck. "So much," he whispers, and then peels away.

He can hear the dull roar of the waterfall from here. And over there, pushed aside on the bed, that silly horror film, playing on Ethan's laptop. By illusion of its flashing luminance, his three-dimensionally extruded mural appears almost animated. Watching the light and the shadows play across its forms, Fox realizes for the first time that it will never be finished, that in time, most likely, the real thing will be painted over, the place converted to a more generic guest bedroom, home office, what have you. Fuck that. Fuck reality. Fox decides he'd rather spend the remainder of his life here, locked inside this most precious memory, even if he can never fix it to unfold the way he'd really like.

"Is this okay?"

"Yes," Fox answers again, as he should have initially. He lays his head onto Ethan's shoulder, nuzzles into Ethan's neck. Another kiss. The scent there—not of cologne, nor of soap, but of living flesh—enraptures Fox. He parts his lips and lingers, finds amusement in a sudden mental image: him as a vampire. He drags his tongue up the salty slope to the ear, takes the lobe gently between his teeth and tugs. His right hand savors its piquant grip on Ethan's. His left slips from its hanging place on Ethan's shirt neck, drops into Ethan's lap, where Fox feels he's had an effect. God, to fuck here, in this confusion of senses. God, to fuck at all. Fox knocks Ethan's head with his own, far less gently than before. "I know you feel me. Why can't you please just say something?"

"Is this okay?"

"Is it okay with you?" Fox dips his fingers into Ethan's waistband, travels until he finds fur, then suddenly recoils, startled by his own transgression. "Sorry, I'm sorry."

Ethan gives him nothing, so Fox releases his hand. He wipes the wet from Ethan's cheek, then from his own.

He gets up to explore, hugs close to the perimeter of the bedroom. His gut tells him to avoid the center, where the blue earth churns in swirls and belches petrichor. It's deeper than it looks, he guesses. Deep enough, probably, to drown. He trudges around to the closet, yanks open its shuddered doors, gouging arced ruts into the vibrant mud. He trades his windbreaker for Ethan's thickest hoodie. Cool, there's his bass guitar, too, and his amp, embedded in the mire. Ethan always got so anxious about people touching his shit, but who's to stop Fox's perusal now?

To the multi-tiered desk, then! A treasure trove of knickknacks and oddities. Many of Ethan's snow globes reside there, including the one Fox modified and gave to him for his fifteenth birthday. His plasma globe's there too. And his drip stick candles. One of the three matching plaster masks Fox made (this one of Pete's face). And lots of books sandwiched between a couple of gargoyle statues. In the top of two drawers, besides school supplies, Fox finds a nugget of fool's gold, a chunk of obsidian, a cord necklace with shark pendant (which he promptly hangs from his neck), several broken seashells, and the most dreadful little souvenir: a snake's rattle.

He draws the second drawer, but it catches on the clay, clears only two or three inches. Enough to spring a rather strange Jack-in-the-box. A half-second delay lapses before Fox's brain processes the image against its indexes and returns an urgent warning: serpent!—more specifically, a monocled cobra—but by then, it's too late. The snake strikes, thwacks its hooded head against Fox's hand! Its rubbery fangs fold against the meat of Fox's palm.

Fox yanks his hand away, realizes the cobra is but an animate toy; its bite, a shock, but otherwise harmless. It pours its coils from the drawer and skims the sludge, etching a sinusoidal wake across the boiling center of the bedroom. Before Fox can ascertain its destination, he feels something lash about his legs. He whips his head back, heart hammering to find more rubber serpents spilling from the desk and biting at his ankles: a coral snake, a banded sea serpent... a rainbow-striped pit viper with a scuffed plastic baby rattle jangling from the tip of its tail? Fox punts the impotent tangle, then kicks Pandora's box shut before it manages to dream up any wilder abominations, kicks it fervently enough to topple the books from the upper shelf. One particularly encyclopaedic volume entitled *The Giant Book of Sea Life For Kids* bangs like a brick against the flat of the desk and fires out a dozen loose-leaf papers that had been tucked inside, scatters them to the core of the bog.

Not thinking, Fox wades after them, sinks within a single step to his thigh; within the next, to his waist. Daring not to venture further, he stretches to collect the pages from the cauldron: crayon drawings, each and every one. Sea creatures, mostly. Fish, octopi, sharks. Their friend from the lagoon: a dopey dayglow hammerhead with sky blue stripes and a comic book speech bubble that reads, ROAAARRRR. Truly not God's creatures, but Ethan's. Not bad drawings either. Too bad that beast isn't half as adorable rendered in flesh and blood as it is in crayon.

Fox hoists himself from the marsh, heads off to the locker room to wash up, then returns spring-fresh to snuggle. He lays Ethan flat, then nestles in, rests his head on Ethan's chest, riding the rise and fall of every breath. He snaps the laptop lid closed with his leg, and begins to drift, listening to the soothing ambience of the distant waterfall... and another sound too, only faintly audible: the beat of Ethan's heart.

Fox wakes in a panic to a screaming alarm: his dutiful, if overzealous, phone insistent to rouse him for school. But where is it? And where is he, he wonders, disoriented to find himself waking... in Ethan's bedroom? Or, kinda. And yeah, there's Ethan. Or, well, kinda. *Oh yeah, he's dead. Oh yeah, the cave.* Last night's a total blur. Fox finds his phone in the side pouch of his boardshorts, shuts off the alarm.

Shit! If he's not home and stirring shortly, his mom'll be checking on him. He leaps from bed, bare feet splashing into wet clay. But wait, no. He told Mom he wasn't going to school. Why shouldn't she just let him sleep? Eh, best not to take the chance. He strips off his borrowed hoodie, tosses it onto the bed.

"I'll be back later," he tells Ethan, grabs his windbreaker, slings his bag over his shoulder, snags his shoes, and takes off hobbling on his bum knee.

The garage door's the quietest, but that would route Fox through the kitchen—the morning hub of the house—to get to the stairs, located in the foyer. Better, he decides, to chance an entrance through the front. He sinks his key into the deadbolt, turns it over ever-so slowly, then lifts up to mute the hinges as he pushes the door in. The place smells strongly of coffee, so Mom's definitely lurking. Fox shuts the door, races up the carpeted steps on all fours, strips off his clothes. By the time he's settled into bed, the exertion's got him coughing, hacking up a lung, hacking up... black phlegm.

Not good. Is that cave ash? No telling how much is inside him, or what it might do to him. But no time to dwell. No sooner does he get his coughing fit under control and his snotty hands wiped on a dirty sock than his mom arrives knocking.

"Come in," he rasps, trying for tired, sounding more ghoulish.

"Whew. It's some kind of ripe in here."

Yikes, yeah, he smells it too. Scent of... *death.* Did he track something home? Or is that his bronchial upchuck stinking so severely?

"Did you get any sleep?"

He covers his mouth in case his breath's the culprit. "A little."

Ma looks at him doubtfully. He knows; he caught a glimpse reflected back at him in the front windows; his face matches the accidental affect of his voice.

"Sure you don't wanna try going back?"

Fox groans and turns over, pulls the quilt over his head.

"Might do good to see your friends."

"What friends?"

"I spoke to Claudia. She said Pete's going."

"Good for him."

"Okay, well. I called school. They said you can make up your exams after break."

"Great."

"You should probably open the windows a while."

"Uh-huh."

"Okay, then. I'm headed out. I'll try and knock off early. Maybe we can watch a movie or something."

"K."

"I love you."

"I love you too," he says flatly, from underneath his shroud.

She shuts him in his sepulcher, taking her warmth with her. If death comes for one of the two of them, it better take him next, because to lose her would be the worst hell imaginable. Why, *why* didn't he look at her beautiful face when he said goodbye?

He blasts out of bed, throws open the door, every intention to bound down the stairs, wrap her tightly in his arms, and make absolute certain she understands just how sincerely he truly does love her, and need her.

But she's already gone.

He returns to his bedroom, stumbles as he shuts the door. He's been on a jet-fueled merry-go-round since he left Ethan's. The vertigo's worse than ever and far slower to subside than after any of his other descents. Probably because he stayed so long, and maybe a little to do with the hangover too... or maybe it's this cave-induced cold he seems to have come down with. He drops to his knees, wilts over the edge of his bed, wishing the place wouldn't make him feel so goddamn dizzy, nauseous.

He coughs again. Dry this time, but he can feel the congestion all through his chest. He breathes into his cupped hands. *Ugh*, yeah, plague breath. He smells the sock he wiped his blackened phlegm onto, gags. Yuh-huh, that's the culprit. Terrifying to think his respiratory system's clogged with more of that shit. What if he gets sick like Ethan? Sick with Ethan?

Good.

Then he'll carry Ethan with him, *in* him, always.

He discards the sock, scratches his collarbone. *Oh yeah, hey.* He tucks chin to chest, fingers Ethan's shark tooth necklace. Totally forgot he stole it; totally forgot Ethan designed Mr. Fishy; totally forgot, *Christ*, that gruesome thing he did with his own younger self. One memory triggers the awful next. *Oh well. Not like the coward didn't have it coming. But yuck, what the hell?*—

The cord is disintegrating, liquifying around his neck, into some kind of black paste. He ventures a whiff. *That's the fucking smell, my god.* The damned thing's rotting, probably from the moment he left the cave with it.

He breaks the cord, chucks the necklace into the trash, wipes his hands and collar with another dirty sock, then disposes of that too, ties the garbage bag shut. Great, but even still, the stench persists, far too potently to ascribe to stained smell receptors.

Oh yeah! The snow globe!

He remembers he fell asleep with it the other night. He dives under his bed, finds it in his phone's usual hiding spot.

The glass dome's withered like a dried pepper, blackened

at its tip. The once-fluorescent roots have gone fully translucent, and brittle. The water's so putrid brown, you can barely even see Ethan or his dad anymore. *Fuck, I forgot to plant you.*

There aren't any empty pots, so Fox tears a handful of succulents from a small ceramic container on the back patio. In their place goes the globe. He cranks the faucet, grabs the hose, wets the soil... then waters his own dehydrated face. As the metallic taste prickles his taste buds, his weary eyelids explode open, sudden inspiration taking him, as usual, by surprise.

NINE

DEEPER, DARKER

Two drippy garden hoses, life jacket, rope, duct tape, several freezer bags, swimming goggles (which he never got to use last time), a refresh of snacks, and a refill of his suicide: these are the supplies Fox has assembled, the ones he's humping down the street towards the woods, drawing the suspicion of old Miss What's-her-name, who used to always invite Fox and Pete in for candy, until they got a little older and decided she was creepy. She had been reading in the shade of her porch when he inadvertently piqued her interest. Not creepy at all, he thinks now, probably just lonely. Maybe a widow, like his mom.

He waves. And she too, in turn. Then she points her nose back into her novel and pretends to resume reading.

Fox drops his haul deep underground in his flooded bedroom, where, one chamber below, he was nearly devoured. Then back up to the grotto, he kneels at the edge of the lagoon. Mr. Fishy's M.I.A. Probably slumbering in the channels of the reef, if sharks slumber. Fox reaches out to claim his floating spear, just *barely* out of reach. He takes a chance and paddles the water to pull it in. Yeah, that alters its drift, but sends it out instead of in. "No, no, come here!" He teeters precariously over the edge, extending his reach.

His wagging fingers hook the handle, and he rakes it in, swiping a swath of pornography in the process, clearing a window through which he glimpses, floating just below the surface, the scattered debris of his partially-devoured double: gnawed limbs, a rope of intestines, and a head that seems to look directly up at Fox. A head that blinks, and emotes.

Fox shrieks and rolls away choking, hacking loose more mucus. He hocks up a big wad of the rancid black slime, spits it onto the carpeted rock shelf.

Mission accomplished: he's got the spear. Only one item remains to collect.

That's Cam. It takes Fox nearly twenty minutes to drag the burly bastard down to his bedroom, shoving him over every drop along the way, to Fox's repeated satisfaction. By the time they arrive, Cam's a sack of broken bones, and Fox aches fiercely in his knee and all through his lower back. He washes a couple of ibuprofen down with a swig of suicide. Double the pain relief.

The final preparations take only moments to complete. He tapes the two hoses into a single length, secures one end to a bedpost, assembling a hundred-foot snorkel. He stuffs Cam into the life jacket, to which he then ties one end of the rope for a leash. The lantern, too big for a single freezer bag, gets one on each end, then taped around the center, and taped to Fox's leg. Phone and keys: into their own freezer bag that Fox then packs into the pouch of his boardshorts.

He thinks of Pete at school, in all those classes where Ethan should be and isn't. First day back, everyone must be asking him about it. Random assholes prob'ly stopping him in the halls, pretending they ever gave a fuck. A scene sets itself in his mind. Some final exam. Chemistry maybe. Pete trying to concentrate. Can't. Keeps looking over at Ethan's empty desk. Fox can only imagine how that must feel. He keeps thinking about Pete's eulogy, what he said about making Ethan laugh. Pete was good at that, getting Ethan to laugh—really laugh—better than Fox was, although not for lack of trying. Mostly, Fox earned participation-point giggles. Ethan was generous that way. That used to make Fox so jealous, that he could never earn the big reaction, made him try all the harder. But thinking 'bout it now, Fox is just glad Pete could do that for him, even if only rarely. *Maybe I should text him*, Fox thinks, *make sure he's okay. But I'd prob'ly interrupt a test, just piss him off. Whatever. He wants to forget, let him try. Hope the whole school harasses him about it. That's what he gets.*

One last swig to calm the nerves.

Shirt off. Shoes too. Goggles on. He muscles Cam to the closet and piles him at the edge, takes the asshole's leash into his left hand, the hose into his mouth, and the spear into his right hand.

The skulls chatter about the walls as if for a better vantage, as if curious what Fox intends to do, or else giddy for his imminent demise.

Deep breath. Now or never.

He punts Cam over the edge and follows into the resulting radiance.

He flips over his knees and flails, inflaming the waters as he kicks, like a frog with lame limbs, burdened by possessions, with tangled streamers of twine and rubber trailing after him. The hose snags, or maybe resists uncoiling. Either way, it's yanked from his mouth, its metal ring grinding his teeth on the way out. He fumbles to grab it before he jets beyond reach... misses with his hand... catches it between his feet, draws it back with the crunch of his stomach. Onward to the bottom, then. He settles into a trench of the snow globe reef, hunkers down in the glow of his leg-lamp, and looks up in awe, as if into outer space, the irradiated clouds and trails birthed by his dive resembling whirling galaxies and nebulas, already cooling to violet and expiring.

He feeds the hose back into his mouth, but his first suck draws a gush of fluid into his throat, lungs, and just about chokes him. There's water in the line. Fox freaks, tries to blow it out the other end, but the hose is too long. Panic very nearly sends him kicking back to the surface. But panic will make a meal of him. *Calm down, calm down*, he convinces himself, and settles on swallowing to clear the line. A couple of gulps do the trick, get him breathing again.

He readies his janky homemade spear, reels the slack out of the rope, every flex sending liquid fireworks pulsing off the line. Cam floats overhead, tethered like a human parade balloon. Fox yanks the leash, makes the bully bob, sundering the darkness with radiating strokes of his contours.

Come and get it.

Seconds pass like eons. And Fox grows only more

anxious in waiting. He gives the leash another tug, sends off another wave of flares.

Where is it, why won't it come?

Fox set the plan in motion the very moment of its conception, never slowed to consider whether or not it would be wise to see through, slave he is to impulse. But crouched among the pulsating snow globes, watching motes drift in and out of the sphere of his lamp's influence, with time dilated by acute terror, he's made and remade his mind up on that matter. The verdict: not wise. Not wise at all.

Still, he *needs* to explore deeper, further, and this was the only way he could figure to do it, with Cam as bait, so he can kill the shark and swim down the passage to that far off shaft of twinkling light, discover where it leads, maybe find an answer to the question that's ruined him: *why?* Yeah, he has some misgivings about destroying Ethan's creatures, but now that he's down here, it's kill or be killed.

So where is the damned thing? Doesn't it smell food?

Blood. That's what it wants. Sharks love that shit.

It's a risk, but he swims up from his shelter, jabs at Cam with his spear, stirring up a firestorm, punching slits that puff red.

The cauldron cools, dims, blackens, without so much as a peep from... wait... *oh, shit*. There it is. Or its ravaged corpse anyway, its polka-dotted head and tail bridged by a rack of spiny cartilage from which scraps of meat flag in the current. A little smaller than the shark in the lagoon above, but no less capable, you'd think, of holding its own in a fight.

So what could do that?

Fox senses a change in his periphery.

There, at the edge of his lamplight, not eight feet away. A reef formation—a jagged humped outcrop, roughly the size of Fox himself—that he's almost pretty certain wasn't there before. Same appearance of sculpted, painted ceramic, but strangely barren of transparent domes and comparatively indistinct in terms of its imagery. Just a vague patchwork of shapes, textures, and colors that seems like it should model some distinguishable memory, and yet somehow doesn't. Studying the perplexing form, Fox realizes it's moving—oozing, really—over the terrain at an almost imperceptible rate, inching itself along on furling and unfurling serpentine appendages, morphing as it goes, reimagining its appearance to better blend with the varied topography, even if it fails in creating comprehensible pictures itself.

An octopus, Fox realizes. And no sooner does he, than the strange cephalopod lifts its pale underside and splays its limbs, presenting itself as an eight-pointed star with a gaping hatch-like maw for a bull's-eye and teeth like curved fish knives.

It launches itself! A streak of white-hot bubbles whizz by Fox's head. The creature affixes itself to Cam, its eight arms coiling like constrictors around the yummy bait, its surface transmuting to match its prey as it unhinges its telescoping jaws and rends a swatch of flesh from bone, polluting the waters with billows of biological murk that light up in fitful strobing flashes like nightmarish storm clouds charged not by lightning, but unsettled plankton.

Fox releases the line, takes the spear into both hands, and thrusts the point up into the beast's cranium. Red fog explodes out of its punctured flesh. Its serpentine arms uncoil from Cam, and it pushes off, splays open, becoming again an eight-pointed star. A defensive display, no doubt. An intimidation tactic, like a cobra flaring its hood.

Oh, shit.

Fox adjusts his grip on his spear.

The creature hovers a moment, graceful as an alien ballerina, then whips its powerful tentacles together with a force like a tidal wave, and streaks off like a comet, leaving a ghost of itself hanging in the dark, and a plasma trail mottled by an expulsion of blood and ink. The resulting undertow sloshes Fox violently within his trench, drags him across the pictorial reef, abrading him with a thousand scrapes and lacerations.

Looking down, he discovers his own puffs of red. He's as good as Cam now. His own bait. He considers breaking for the surface.

No.

It would take too long to heave himself from the water; that's when it would get him, latch onto him with its horrid suckers and yank him into the depths, never to be seen or heard from again... or else follow him to dry land, overtake him there. Didn't Ethan send him a video once of a small octopus doing just that to a crab?

Calm down, calm down. It's just calamari. You're a man. Most fearsome predator that ever lived.

He hunkers back down into position.

Wait, no way, there are Pete's keys. Gleaming in the dimming violet blush of the plankton. He quickly grabs 'em, stuffs 'em into the side pouch of his boardshorts, then readies his spear as the waterway blackens outside the glow of his lantern.

He spots the beast way back in the shadows, with eyes like disembodied orbs, reflecting his lamplight right back at him.

Come on, bitch. I'll cut you up and cook you over lava, have your tentacles for dinner.

He tugs Cam's line, shoots off more tantalizing flares.

The eyes disappear.

And with them, Fox's bravado.

He notices that the knife at the tip of his spear's wobbling like a loose tooth. That's gonna take the bite out of his next strike. He might be able to pull off one more jab, if he's lucky.

And what if he does manage to defeat the octopus? What if he swims down to that twinkling shaft of light, finds it to be—like those Psychic Brine videos—a supreme disappointment, without secrets to be uncovered? Maybe some things are better left a mystery.

He checks the surface again. Could he make it?

Not likely.

Why the hell did I do this? I just wanna be up there, eating Oreos and getting drunk.

Is it his imagination, or is the darkness eating at the perimeter of his lamplight? Is his lantern dimming? He casts a glance at his scraped leg, where it resides. Difficult to tell for sure. Either way, he curses himself for failing to think to trade the batteries.

Glittering light draws Fox's gaze ahead just as the shooting star, spread-eagle as if for a hug, verges upon his face, mouth agape to flaunt its rows of curved blades.

Fox screams bubbles, blows the life support from his mouth. His arms butterfly up to propel him down; he bends backwards to play limbo, narrowly avoids the jaws, but a suckered whip lashes his face, breaking the seal of his right goggle cup, which instantly fills with salty water, and blinding ink. A fresh expulsion blots out any trace of light, swallows Fox into murky palls that utterly disorient him. He strokes his arms and kicks his feet, not altogether certain whether he's pointed up or down.

He bangs his chin hard on the bottom, feels his way into the trench, and flattens himself on his back as the beast strikes again, crashing itself down on the reef in an explosion of wisping sparks, shattering a dozen or more snow globes as it squirms and thrashes, grabbing at Fox with its serpentine arms, gobbling at him with its razor maw.

Fox sticks it.

It flails, morphs, redesigns its cranium to sport a stoney human visage with a half dozen horns: the mask Fox cast from Ethan's face. It takes hold of the spear with a spiraling grip, breaks the knife from the broom handle and sends it jetting as it threshes its appendages and rockets into the shadows.

Christ, am I killing a part of Ethan? Fox panics. *What if I can't even kill it? What if it can't die?* He thinks of his own dismembered double in the lagoon above, still living, even after decapitation. *I'm dead.* No depth perception, no weapon, no air. No hope for survival. He checks out the surface again, beyond Cam's shredded, and yet still animated cadaver. Could he make it?

No chance.

Panning desperately for other options, he spots the gleaming kitchen knife, maybe six or seven feet away... the hose, further even than that... Cam's tether, on the other hand, dangles just beyond reach. Okay, he has an idea, but he's rapidly running out of breath.

He bats the rope in with his broom handle, threads the line through a loop in the coral, then uses it like a pulley to draw Cam down... down... down... to him.

Dumb invertebrate takes the bait, torpedoes the carcass, draws it into a constricting embrace, and goes to town, tearing it asunder. Fox releases the line, lets Cam float like a gory balloon, by the buoyancy of his life vest, swiftly back to the surface, the entangled octopus riding along, feasting the entire way.

Fox propels himself in a glaring streak of light across the seafloor, grabs the knife.

Last chance to live.

He kicks off the reef and attacks, sinks his blade in and out and in and out—a storm of flashing amber—punching the bloated cranium with a dozen blood-spewing vents.

The tentacles slacken, and the beast sags, unravels from Cam and plummets like a falling star, crash-landing atop the coral, where it flounders pathetically, severely (if not mortally) wounded. Its surface mutates, flushes with color and varied textures, a pathetic attempt to hide itself among the patchwork pictography.

Fox breaks the surface and gasps, chokes for much-needed breath. A difference of seconds would have seen him drowning. He pulls himself up out of the closet, beaches himself on the flooded floor of his bedroom, panting and coughing in alternating wheezes, trembling wildly, surging with adrenaline. He roars and beats his chest like an ape.

Exposed to fresh air, his lacerated arms, legs, and back cry out in stinging agony and spit watery red rivulets over his slick body. He grabs the liquid painkiller and turns it up.

Looking over the edge, he can barely make out the camouflaged beast on the seafloor below. It looks back up with pleading orbs that overwhelm Fox with a great swell of shame, pity.

He adjusts his goggles and dives back in to finish the job before he loses his nerve.

Pete lines up with the horde of kids filing into school from the portables, where he just aced his Spanish final. The left of the twin doors is locked to outside access, exacerbating the usual bottleneck. Several kids tug the handle to confirm. Only one, once through, thinks to help the others. A dude in a Dead Kennedys shirt and combat boots turns around and kicks the bar, punching the door open with a violent thwack against the tightly packed throng of teenage bodies. The door seals shut again before anyone can catch it. Far off thunder rumbles across the tarmac. Pete looks up into the grey. Great migrating mountains of charcoal and obsidian gather... lightning flashes, then bangs, loudly enough to elicit shrieks. The mosh pit compresses, shoulders jostling, threatening to tip him off his feet as students shove their way to shelter. Once through, Pete makes his own effort to relieve the congestion, but the inflowing tide barricades the door. Oh well.

Off to second period: chemistry, last review session before tomorrow's exam. He finds himself dragging, the closer he gets. Ethan should be there. It's the first of three classes they shared. But there's only so much length to the halls, only so long he can put it off.

He loiters outside the door, uncommitted to entering as he peeks in at the empty desk. Several students, already settled, look up from their books, spot him. You can practically hear the questions breeding in their minds.

He backs away...

Ducks into the south stairwell just as the bell sounds, slumps to a seat under the steps where this girl, Bex Meyer, was rumored to have been caught giving head to a senior, first week back from summer break. Crude graffiti commemorates the alleged occasion. Pete pulls out his phone, taps out a text to Fox: *You exploring?*

He studies the message before shooting it off, anxiety wreaking havoc on his pulse as his imagination parades a panoply of Fox's most probable responses, none good. He stares until the letters stop making sense, then erases them.

With the guardian of the further reaches defeated, oxygen flowing freely through his rubber umbilical line, and his knife now taped to his hip, just in case, Fox takes his time crawling along the bottom, lantern illuminating the memories stored in the pulsating globes. Birthdays, Christmases, Halloweens. School settings and vacations. Childhood soccer games. A first concert. A school play. Friendships come and gone. Weird to think that any one person would only know Ethan by the small percentage of scenes they shared. But not Fox. He can see himself forty years on, in a brimmed hat and cargo pants, the archaeologist of Ethan's life, still working with a spade and a brush to uncover it all, to learn Ethan as well as he knew himself.

The further he goes, the more unsettled the waters become, with hydrothermal vents jetting hot and cool streams, oppositional currents churning fierce turbulence against which Fox has to abandon his sightseeing to contend. Swimming harder and harder, he becomes ever more aware that the walls are closing in, constricting the passage to a cramped duct, diameter of about four feet. The climate here proves inhospitable to life. The plankton cease to phosphoresce. The snow globes wither and rot, palpitating irregular diseased rhythms, pumping blood, guts, and putrescence, some infested by cockroaches. Pale, translucent roots fan wide, seeking more viable accommodations, threading vast webs that threaten to ensnare Fox. The migrating globes leave gaping apertures that bleed like the gum-sockets of pulled teeth. As he draws nearer the shimmer, strength flagging, Fox gets the feeling he's being digested, wonders if the light at the end of the tunnel might prove to be a lure, meant to draw him willingly down the cave's gullet.

A sudden snag yanks the snorkel, but he bites down hard, grasps the hose and gives several good tugs to whip it free, then paddles on.

Drawing closer now, he can lay his fears to rest. The light's not shed by a lure but a watery portal, as he had hoped, bespeckled and marbleized by eddying swaths of floating coal dust.

He surfaces through the powdery skim and hoists himself onto a shelf of filthy carpeted clay, collapses, utterly exhausted, relieved for a moment's rest. He spits out the breathing tube and pats it into a mud cake for safe keeping, then rips off his goggles, shakes out his hair, and rears, panting, onto his knees to claim the fruit of his adventuring, to plunder the cave's most precious pearl, its most guarded memory.

Ethan's bedroom. Buried underneath the blanketing ashen precipitation of some nuclear winter, hazy with stratified bands of immiscible smog and ozone layers, and bathed in the bleaching sulfurous glow of the yellow-grey pulsar imprisoned in the grime-encrusted ceiling-fan dome along with a living scrim of skittering cockroaches that filter the output into a flickering shadow play, projecting a phantasmagoric scourge about the trickle-eroded walls of the apocalyptic chamber, the sieved incandescence bolstered by the fizzing fountain-like road-flare flames shooting out of three drip stick candles, and bolstered by Fox's leg-strapped lantern (waning now to an almost negligible contribution). Across the room, two tar-dust-flocked figures—Ethan and Fox, presumably, although they look more like moldering mummified bog bodies—huddle together cross-legged and holding hands in the fluffy soot that's accreted atop a bed concealed entirely by cascading berms of ash.

Fox puckers his lips and empties his lungs at the boys but succeeds only in stirring up a storm of particulate, which he immediately chokes on.

He kneels and cups his hand to one of many stagnating puddles that riddle the marshy dimpled surface of the balding carpet and exposed substrate. He carries the dripping bowl to Ethan and gently bathes the face, bringing to light the pink flesh and delicate features he so adores, streaked with stubborn mascara stains. Fox scrubs these with his thumbs.

The cleansed face ripples with consternation. The jaw gapes, gasps, then speaks. "Can I tell my dad about us?"

"No," bog-Fox begs, puffing the carbon that still blackens his countenance.

The real Fox's hands shoot up to his head, grab fistfuls of his hair as a strange stuttering whine chirps out of him, something that maybe started as a groan, but got constricted, mangled in his pipes. *Not this, please. I can't take it.*

"Are you embarrassed?" Ethan asks, after a lengthy silence.

"No," the two Foxes answer at once, the real one with a good deal more conviction than the other seems capable of mustering.

"I understand if you are."

"I'm not. I just..." the Fox clone huffs soot, frustrating himself with a total failure of words.

I was never embarrassed by you. I was just embarrassed by me.

"It's okay. I won't tell anyone. I like having this part of you to myself."

Fox's legs give; he drops into the mire, head lolling like a heavy weight, the sparse few hairs of his unshaven chin scratching his chest. Blood trickles in diluted yellow-red streaks down his glistening lacerated back. He sweeps his dripping hair back off his forehead. *Why didn't I just let you? I should have let you tell him.*

The memory loops. "Can I tell my dad about us?" Ethan asks again.

"I'll tell him, I promise," *I'll tell everyone.*

As if cued by the declaration, the cave begins to rumble, softly at first, then violently enough to rattle knick-knacks and oscillate puddles. Black matter sheds from the fan blades in heavy palls. The lower waterway sloshes from its banks and washes across the floor, lapping at Fox. He springs back to his feet, braces himself against a bare patch of craggy wall, where an anemic trickle washes his bare freckled shoulders with icy snaking rivulets. Books tumble from the desk. The wandering night table tips, dumps a drip stick candle into the swash; the torch burns straight to the bottom, impregnates the pool with sputtering light. The ceiling fan dome cracks under the tremoring stress, and sprung cockroaches flee in pulsing waves as the gaseous luminance seeps out in cascading swells, like vapor from dry ice, adhering to an inverted sense of gravity as it flows, dissipates across the popcorn ceiling, charging a universe of paste-on stars before abandoning the task of illumination to them, and to the remaining drip stick flares, plus the meager contribution of Fox's dying lantern. The ground shears underfoot, fragments into carpeted plates that buckle near the mouth of the waterway, cave into the swill, taking the snorkel along. Fox hurls himself from the wall as a giant fissure shoots like a bolt of lightning across the porous surface, blowing out the grimy window. He splats down atop the sodden slab, folds his arms behind his head just as the tremors cease.

He keeps his head tucked until well after the rattling ceases before he decides, finally, to risk a peek at the carnage. Easing out of hiding, sitting up onto his knees, he finds half the room crumbled like a sand castle. Behind him, the gashed wall whistles like an arctic gale, sucking breath into a boxy horizontal shaft where the window had been.

Come in, come see, it seems to invite. *Come deeper.*

But even light dares not enter. Not beyond three or four feet. Inside: a mineralized passage stratified into layers of cerulean, periwinkle, and robin's egg, cleaved into jagged shale-like flakes, recedes to a blackness that seems somehow deeper than utter. Fox stares long into the rectangular abyss, expecting his eyes to adjust and expose its secrets, but they never do.

He turns away, crawls on hands and knees to the collapsed lip of the waterway. Completely dammed by sunken debris, hardly any deeper now than a kiddy pool. *No-no, shit.* He dives into the mini-quarry, thrashes feverishly, futilely to clear the piled rubble, every ticking second without success supercharging his dread, making a desperate fumbling wreck of him. He draws his knife from its duct-tape holster at his hip, wedges it deep between two boulders, wins some leverage... then the blade snaps. Fox cries out, hurls the useless handle across the room.

An aftershock makes a jangling tambourine of the murky bedroom. Looking up at the clattering fan and the fracture lines shot out from it, Fox wonders how many tons of earth bear down on him, how many feet divide him from daylight. What if he never sees it again? Never feels it on his back, nor his face, suffusing him with its life-giving warmth? No one even knows where he is. Pete may surmise, but even if he comes looking, even if (and it's a big if) he'd be willing to brave the waterway to find Fox, what could he do? He takes out his ziplocked phone. No signal, of course. Not this far underground.

He checks out the cleaved wall, that sucking rectangular throat.

He climbs out of the rubble, snags one of the fountaining drip stick flares, flings it deep into the shadows. The resilient flame—impervious even to water—sputters and gasps, dies, doused by darkness.

The hell?

He takes up the last remaining candle, carries it to the shaft, and points the spewing tip just into the shade...

The shadows gobble the flame, and then surge forth to take the bedroom, snuffing first the pale green universe above, and then Fox's leg-lamp.

He feels his way to the inlet and hoists himself into it. What choice does he have but to continue on?

Deeper... deeper... into a lung-coating atmospheric malaise, feeling his way through squeezes and corkscrews... barometric fluctuations deadening his hearing, blood pooling in his face, telling him he's trending down, not up, not out. He forces a yawn to equalize his inner ear pressure, only manages to unclog his left. Through it comes the rasp of a dying boy. Fox shudders at the thought of some phantom pursuer before recognizing the source as his own throat, apparently performing an imitation of the horrid fleshwind tune he pumped out of Ethan that day at the creek. His lungs are so polluted, his pipes so constricted, he draws breath in strangled whistles and wheezes.

Deeper... deeper, still... has it been moments or hours? Maybe years? Feels like an eternity. *This is what it must have been like every day, every minute in Ethan's mind. No wonder,* Fox almost, *almost* allows himself to think. Then a teal-blue strobe goes off like a camera flash, washing him with frigid light, decorating his flesh with glittering ice crystals, which his body heat instantly thaws.

Onward, his proximity triggers another subzero flash. He sees briefly the cloud of his breath, and beyond, a stretch that veers leftward before him, the glistening indigo shale overgrown by a denser and denser mat of orange friendship mycelium from which sporadic Cold Lights flower... then the shadows gush to swallow him, and is it his imagination, or do they swirl into ghastly specters? Does he discern faces among them? Whispering, murmuring faces? Does he feel lips pressed to his ear? Warm, moist tickling breath?

Do it right here, after they go. Might as well.

Fox knows that voice. Knows it well.

"Ethan?"

When no answer comes, he paws on, fingers all pins and needles. Another foot, another flash that pricks his face with barbs of ice, chills his welling eyes so severely, he has to clamp his lids to warm them.

Another voice molests his left ear: *While you're still young.*

And his pressure-muffled right: *While there's still something romantic about it.*

The freezer burn has yet to defrost from his eyelashes, brows, or downy forearms before, inching on, he sparks another flash, and another, and another; the Cold Lights trigger each other, go off like a mob of paparazzi; he, a celebrity, newly arrived at some red-carpet event.

Blood as thick as slush, he draws his extremities to his bare core, hugs himself tight, shivering violently as a blizzard precipitates from the moist smog.

The lights, like old-timey flash bulbs, get but one pop each, and soon the entire garden's spent, the passage taken once more by utter darkness. A voice cuts through Fox's quivering, panting gasps—

Don't be a pussy, just do it.

"Why are you doing this?" Tears skate Fox's icy cheeks and crystalize. He commands his body to action, but his body forsakes him, too ravaged finally to carry him even another inch. His thoughts travel once again to Pete, remembering how effortlessly he dispelled the darkness during Fox's mushroom trip. Must have been the same for Ethan, with those jokes that elicited big laughter. If only he was here now.

His light! Fox remembers, and manages with considerable effort to roll himself onto his back. He snakes a quaking hand down to his shorts, fishes Pete's keyring from his pocket, jams the button—

A searing beacon blasts into the pitch, and the shadows disperse, skittering like the frightened pests they are.

As if drawn to the glow, bristling friendship fibers stand up and strain to tickle Fox with their caresses, from Fox's furry shins to his abraded torso and all along the folded left arm that props him up.

This *is* Ethan.

Knew it before, but now he's sure of it. These roots, this cave. Every inch. Even the shark, octopus. Protective instinct. Animal instinct. But these roots are Ethan as Fox remembers him: gentle, affectionate, nurturing.

This is Ethan.

He splays his fingers, and the fibers entwine his digits, as if to hold hands.

"You want me to die?" *If so, I will.* "You want me to come with you?"

A voice reverberates out from the baying shadows: Ethan's. It comes to Fox via his ears and his scalp; it resonates every last hair on his body.

I wish... I wish for Fox to find a way to be as happy as he used to be.

A sudden splash of radiance lights Fox up like a ghost, suffuses his flesh with life-giving warmth.

Sunlight.

Looking up, he finds a newborn shaft flaring open to the glow of day. Already, he can feel his trembling body beginning to thaw.

He climbs.

And as he does, the mycelium weaves webs underneath him, suspending tiers upon tiers of safety netting. Once and only once, he loses his footing, but the filaments catch him, boost him onward to the surface...

He breaches not twelve feet away from where Ethan departed, not twelve feet from the dig and the Sphincter of Madness. As he climbs from the earth, the shaft seals shut behind him.

A shroud of gloom bears down, but sunrays break through. Casting his face to the sky, Fox revels in the healing glow.

At home, he heads around back to check on his souvenir snow globe: perished, he finds, to his profound regret, planted too late to save. The corroded dome has ruptured and, except for a swampy brown pool of the stuff stagnating at the bottom, the water's drained out into the soil. The putrescing flesh figurines—Ethan and his dad at Pride—stink fiercely of spoiled meat. Fox disposes of the mess and goes on into the house, reminded of his promise.

I'll tell him. I'll tell everyone.

He hasn't got the strength to stand, so he sits in the tub, fresh water spraying over him. The steam breaks up his congestion. He keeps coughing up fizzy dark spitwads that run like ribbons toward the drain. He uses his right pointer finger to trace the blurry teal lines running through his scratched up left forearm.

It can't have been easy.

He towels off, applies several band-aids, then checks into his room long enough to change into dry clothes, but *these skulls*, perfumed fittingly by the lingering scent of death... and, *my god*, the way the cave's persisting psychotropic influence animates their proportions and perspectives, twists them into funhouse monstrosities, at least when he stares too long. But how can he not?

Back downstairs, then. Late afternoon. Rain patters the windows. He turns up the heat. Few hours to kill before his mom returns home. Maybe they can watch a movie or something, like she said. He's had enough memory-mining for now. He considers busting what's left of his suicide out of his bag, but that's not what he wants either. Not now that he's sobering up.

He lies belly down on the cold leather couch where his dad died. Some might find that morbid. Fox finds it comforting. He slept there for weeks after that terrible night last spring. Belly down, like now. Closest he could get to a hug from his dad. Closest he could get to his dad, period. The sofa's pretty much gone disused since then, a constant reminder of the terrible vacancy in their lives, his and his mother's. She mentioned possibly replacing it once, but Fox wouldn't hear of it. Been a long, long time since he's lain there, but right now, he just needs to feel close to his dad again. He drags the throw from the spine, wraps himself up.

I killed an octopus today, he reminds himself, mentally mapping his new discoveries so he won't forget. *Oh yeah, I was gonna look for some videos about caving*. But the fact is, today's journey, and especially that final memory, really killed his desire to explore. Maybe he doesn't want to know definitively for sure if he's to blame for Ethan's death. Maybe, taken together, he's found proof enough he is. Already, he's having trouble figuring how he could possibly carry on one more day, two, a week under the crushing weight of all this guilt, let alone the entire rest of his life. If he'd only known the extent of Ethan's suffering.

I wish for Fox to find a way to be as happy as he used to be.

That plays again and again in his head. *Happy? How could I be happy?*

His stomach growls. Except for a few cookies, he hasn't eaten a thing all day. He considers getting up to microwave some frozen pizza rolls, but his body refuses to even entertain the thought.

Pete's probably home by now. If he doesn't have practice. Wonder if he checked the mail.

Ears plugged, music blasting, Pete's just finishing his fifth set of bicep curls in front of his closet mirror, exhausting the angst of a bitter day, when his mom enters.

"Found this in the mailbox," she says in her heavy accent and drops a letter onto his desk.

"¿Qué es?"

"No sé," she says and leaves.

Pete sets down the weights, sweeps back his sweat-dampened hair, and takes up the envelope: marked simply *Pete* in big scraggly letters, drawn so forcefully the pen tip carved grooves. Pete tears the flap and out spring his keys.

Jesus, Fox. How did you get these?

Fox is conked out by the time his mom arrives home. Discovering him there on his dad's couch shakes her up like one of Ethan's snow globes, stirs the sediment of last spring's storm, silt not long settled. She kneels beside him, pets his hair. She doesn't intend to wake him, just wants to be there for him, with him. But wake he does.

"You're home," he says hoarsely.

"What happened?" She's spotted the band-aids.

"Fell, skating."

"Hungry?"

"Yeah."

"I was gonna make a calzone, can you wait?"

Big grin. Yeah, he can wait for his favorite food in the world.

"Go back to sleep, I'll wake you." She heads into the kitchen.

"Do we have any Mucinex or anything?" he asks, rousing.

"Did you check the drawer?"

"No."

"There might be something like that in there. I hope you're not coming down with a cold."

"Me too."

"Check the drawer. I'll go out if we don't have anything."

Rifling through the home pharmacy, he discovers an old antibiotic prescription bottle made out to his dad. After all this time, it still stings to find little things like that. He selects from several cold and flu options.

"Did we have anything?" his mom asks, upon his return.

"Uh-huh."

"Oh, good." She scours the utensil drawer, then checks the dishwasher.

"What're you lookin' for?"

"Have you seen the good knife?"

Fox gulps. *Uh*, "No."

She settles on an older serrated blade, washes it, grabs some vegetables from the crisper.

Fox hangs on the bar, watches her while he works up some nerve. "Mom?"

"Huh?"

Tell her, tell her. "I have to tell you something."

"What is it?"

Why's it so fucking hard? Just tell her. "Nothing."

She stops chopping, gives him her full attention. "No, tell me. What?"

He shrinks under the twin spotlights of her expectant gaze. He hangs his head, picks at the sticker on one of the apples in the fruit bowl. "Do you still think about Dad?"

"Every day."

"Me too."

"We were so lucky to have him."

"Yeah." He gets the sticker off, stamps it down on the counter with his thumb... then starts picking at it again. "What do you think if I go back to school tomorrow?"

"That would be fine. If that's what you wanna do. Which tests do you have?"

"Government, I think. And Biology."

"You feel up to it?"

He sighs. "I dunno."

"It's up to you."

So, *okay*. The magic's gone. Exhausted. Wrung out. Or maybe it's that he destroyed the mystique when he lit up the darkness and found the videos lacking. Either way, these

Psychic Brine songs are so flat and lifeless, Fox can't believe they ever did anything for him at all.

He yanks the earbuds out and turns over. He thinks about all the things he might have hidden in the dark. A black skull maybe, animated to perform the lyrics. An endoscopic view of a mouth... or a womb... or a rectum. A swarm of daddy longlegs. A swarm of cockroaches. A trip through the darkest parts of Ethan's cave. That would be cool especially if YouTube had a night vision button and you could click it on and off, alternate between green and black, between something and nothing. What would be really cool is if you could print videos or GIFs so that they're animated on paper. Maybe if that was possible he'd video himself kissing his favorite Ethan-thing (the one that's always checking in, asking if it's okay to be holding his hand for the first time), print out the clip, and conceal the action with black crayon, so that someone would have to go at it with fingernails to reveal his secret. Maybe he'd make a card like that. A bunch of them. Send one to everyone he knows. He wonders how many people would take it at face value, and how many would be curious enough to scratch the surface, find the color underneath. *Guess I could do it with a regular picture*, he thinks. *That'd be such a weird way to come out.*

Pete's not at the bus stop, and Fox isn't sure whether he should feel relieved or disappointed about that. He's only guessing but he has an image in his mind of Summer driving Pete—in a convertible, even though he knows her car isn't—radio blasting, wind in their hair, Pete with his feet kicked up on the dash, both just a'smiling and laughing. Boy, what a sun-shining day. At least in their world. Fox's mom offered him a ride so he wouldn't have to wait out in this freezing drizzle. He said no. Mostly because he wanted to sit with Ethan's absence. And maybe a little because he wanted to see Pete. Part of him's maybe hoping they could make up. Whether they do or don't now is really Pete's prerogative. Lunch will tell, if he returns to the table the three boys once shared or if he's truly done and moving on. But if Fox is really honest about his motivations, it's more to do with wanting to hurt Pete a little, haunt him, so Pete can't just easily forget. So yeah, *okay*, Fox is disappointed. But who needs friends anyway when you've got a booze medley for company? He ditched the plastic water bottle for an opaque thermos before heading out, filled it to the brim with a little of everything, assuming no one would be the wiser. The brew's warming him now while he waits alone for his ride.

Some minutes later, he's some morbid brand of celebrity boarding a yellow stretch limousine filled with fans and paparazzi. That, or he's some kind of novelty act. Either way, he can't stand the scrutiny, can't stand all the stolen glances over seatbacks. He flips his hood, puts in his earbuds and cues Death Caves, watches rivulets streak the window pane while he poisons his liver.

In the halls, he's a nobody. Just like always. Nobody knew Ethan. Nobody knows him. They only know some kid killed himself. *Whatever. More oxygen for everyone else.* Or so he overheard some girl say. Closest he sees to any kind of memorial is a hand-painted banner advertising Suicide Hotline. Ethan deserves better, but frankly Fox is glad not to have his face rubbed in it.

Cutting through the herd, Fox crosses paths with Pete, and Pete gets this look like... yeah, like Fox is some kind of specter or something. It's not just surprise to see him. It feels more like revulsion, with a twist, perhaps, of concern.

"Hey?" Pete says.

Fox ignores him, keeps walking, thinking surely Pete'll pursue, at least if he's any kind of friend.

"Fox!"

Fox doesn't so much as turn his head.

And no, Pete doesn't pursue.

First exam of the day: government. On top of everything else, Fox is feeling like a moron, because he doesn't know *any* of the answers. Fifteen minutes in, he just gives up, slumps over his desk, head down. He just keeps thinking how much he wants to go to bed. Not his, but Ethan's, in his favorite memory.

Lunch is the nightmare he imagined. Ethan's absence is palpable. A black hole. And Pete's made up his mind, apparently, washed his hands of the two of them. He's within eyeshot, few tables over, sitting with Summer and his lacrosse buddies, including Jay, who he always tried to set Ethan up with, and, would you believe, Cam fucking Ford. Oh, and great. Here comes Summer.

"Hey," she says, and helps herself to Ethan's seat.

Fox yanks out one of his earbuds. "Hey."

"I've tried to call you a bunch of times."

Yeah, *I know.* "Why?"

"Make sure you're okay."

"I'm fine."

"Come sit with us."

"Why?"

"We want you to."

"Pete doesn't."

"Yeah, he does."

"Then why doesn't he come say so?"

"Somebody's gonna smell that." She means Fox's suicide. He just took a swig.

"What?" Fox wipes his mouth.

She lowers her voice just shy of a whisper. "I know about you and Ethan." She places her hand on his.

He yanks away. *The fuck do you know? You don't know anything.*

"Please come sit with us," she says, with an unseemly amount of compassion, as if she was talking him off a ledge or something.

Fox sniffles and draws his hand into his hoodie sleeve, wipes the wet rims of his nostrils. He glances at their table. Pete's engaged in conversation, feigning disinterest in Summer's efforts, but he keeps looking this way. "*He* doesn't want me to," Fox reiterates.

"He's the one who told me to come get you."

Somehow Fox doubts that. And even if Pete did put her up to it, so what, because there's no way in hell Fox is gonna sit over there with Cam. And he couldn't possibly abandon Ethan's seat anyway. If Pete was any kind of friend at all—to Fox or to Ethan—he'd come back, join Fox here.

"Come on," she says and hooks his arm, rises, tugging him along.

He tears free. "Just leave me alone," he practically shouts. "I'm fine here."

"Okay, I'm sorry." She relents but then lingers, giving him a chance to change his mind. He doesn't. He catches his dangling earbud and plugs his ear. "I'll see you in art," she says, and off she goes.

Fox locks eyes with Cam, who's got a big doofy grin plastered across his face.

Cam lifts his chin: *what's up?*

Fox snarls, turns up his thermos.

The world's a delicate clockwork, a perpetual motion machine with human cogs grinding endlessly against one another. Some minor catastrophe, in the scheme of things, broke Fox out of alignment. These other students, teachers —*God, everyone* just keeps on ticking, but he's stuck out of time. *I don't belong here,* he realizes, trading books at his locker. *I should be home with Ethan.* He's giving some serious thought to calling his mom and asking her to please come pick him up when he suddenly senses a predator in his periphery.

"Hey, man," Cam says and tips his considerable mass against the lockers.

Fox decides not to give him the courtesy of naked ears. If Cam wants to talk, he'll have to defeat the decibels of Death Caves.

"I just wanted to say... I'm sorry about Ethan."

Fox stares at him in disbelief.

"I was wondering," Cam scratches his elbow. "Did he give any kind of reason, or—"

"What?" The earbuds come out. Maybe he didn't hear right. Couldn't have.

"I was so shitty to him last year, to both of you. I really regret that, man. I was just going through a bunch of shit, you know, and, I'm not trying to make excuses, but I really wish I could take it all back. I dunno, I guess I just keep worrying that I maybe might have had something to do with—"

"Are you fucking serious?" Fox cuts him off, pulse racing, vein pounding violently in his forehead. "You think he did this 'cause of you?"

Cam seems to sense he's done more harm than good, puts his hands up as if to show he means no harm. "Sorry.

Sorry, man. I just wanted to say—Well, just that, I'm sorry." And off he goes, freed of his burden.

Fox can't just let it go, can't just let that fucker walk away unscathed, can't just cower shamefully like he did all last year when he let Cam say and do all those terrible things to Ethan. He's not the same loathsome coward he was then. No, he's a motherfucking tomb raider now. He dumps his backpack onto the floor.

A cluster of chatting girls shriek and scatter as the boys sprawl headlong through them, hurdling into a row of lockers.

Cam recovers quickly, turns to face his assailant. "You're fucking dead."

He launches himself at Fox, inspiring a new round of screams. Students fumble to clear a path as the brawlers careen towards the opposite wall. Fox loses his footing, chips the back of his head off the latch of one of the lockers and drops between shuffling, stampeding legs as Cam—a great toppling tower of muscle—catches himself with an outstretched arm and manages to stay upright.

Slumped underneath the straddling colossus, Fox snakes his fingers through his messy hair, 'round to the back of his skull, and finds dampness. He examines his blurry digits through dim, splotchy vision: wet with traces of blood. The bell sounds, warning the cattle to herd along, but the whine's higher pitched than usual and cranked loud enough, for whatever reason, to cause severe hearing damage. Or is that not the bell, but Fox's ears ringing?

Cam slugs Fox woozy, bounces his head like an inverted speedball-type punching bag. Again, and again. Temple, cheek, brow.

"Stop!" some girl screeches, horrified by the brutality.

And there's the actual bell, but no one heeds it. Instead, they gather, encircle the action as Fox makes a futile attempt to knock Cam off his feet.

Pete's just parted company with Summer and plotted course for fifth period when he hears the chants and jeers, sees kids running, flocking to the fight. He follows...

The kids in the back spring on tippy toes, climb on lockers, desperate for a look. One of them's RJ, the annoying-as-shit little mop-headed freshman from their bus. "It's Fox," he says, beaming, then adds with great relish, "He's getting his ass kicked."

Oh, shit.

Pete wedges himself through the onlookers.

Cam's just about to deliver another blow when Pete blasts out of the crowd, grabs hold and flings the bastard, his own weight following through, sending he and Cam both flailing, flesh and rubber soles smearing along the tile, producing a series of stuttering chirps so terrible all the spectators simultaneously and audibly cringe.

Yeah, Pete's quite a bit bigger and stronger than Fox, but the difference is negligible compared to Cam's bulk, so no surprise who gets the upper hand. Pete suffers several blows to the face and only manages to return one of his own before administrators break through the crowd and intervene.

They look pretty raw, these two who once were brothers, sitting across from each other in the front office with faces like storm clouds, puffy and purplish. Pete spits blood into a wad of brown paper towels. He bore the brunt of Cam's wrath, it seems, took the worst of Fox's beating for him. The victor is with one of the assistant principals, painting a portrait of victimhood, the boys can hear, even through the closed door. Any moment, their mothers will be here, a thought so anxiety-inducing, Pete can't keep his leg from jackhammering the floor. He keeps fretting about suspension, expulsion, his remaining finals, getting cut from the team, all the worst possible outcomes he can imagine.

Fox can't fathom how any of that means anything to Pete at all when Ethan's fucking ashes now. Ashes and memories. And where are the ashes anyway? In an urn on a mantle? Or scattered in nature somewhere? He may never know. He doesn't even know where his own dad's remains are. His mom didn't want to bring them home right away, couldn't bear it, for whatever reason he couldn't quite comprehend. He didn't put up a fight, although he hated the idea of leaving them at the funeral home. They never went back to claim them. Fox worries they might have been discarded by now. He's been too afraid to ask. "I didn't need your help," he tells Pete. He doesn't need the extra guilt to carry.

"Yeah, that's why we both got our asses kicked."

"I didn't *want* your help."

"Seriously? Dude, what the fuck is your problem?"

"Why did you tell Summer about me and Ethan? It's none of her fucking business."

"I didn't."

"Yes, you fucking did."

"I swear to you, I didn't."

"Then how does she know?"

"She just guessed."

"What did you say?"

"What does it matter? She doesn't care."

"Then why say anything?"

"I didn't tell her."

They stew in silence a long while, each boy refusing to look at the other, Pete continuing to spit blood.

"How'd you get my keys?"

"I told you I would."

"Yeah, but what about the shark?"

"Wasn't a shark, it was an octopus. I killed it."

"Serious?"

Fox shrugs, cool.

"Where does it go? Is there a lot more?"

"Thought you didn't wanna know."

Pete sighs. "I don't."

"Your loss."

"It doesn't make you sick? Being down there?"

Sick as a fucking dog. Sick as death, but, "It makes me feel close to him."

"We have to tell his parents."

"Why?"

"It's fucking wrong to keep it to ourselves."

"No."

"They have a right to see it."

"I said no."

"I hope you're happy," Fox's mom says, then cranks down the radio and pins him with one hell of an evil eye. He sinks low in the passenger seat. He's been suspended. Pete too. They're not sure yet if they'll get to make up their exams, even though the school said before he could. His return apparently somehow nullifies that, not that he could give a damn. He twists to see out the side window.

The world races by, but Fox throws it out of focus by zeroing in on the rain droplets. He watches one chase another down the diagonal path the first forges across the glass. It seems the follower may never catch the pioneer, but it suddenly picks up speed, jets forward and collides with the original, melding the two into one. "Yeah, real fucking happy, Mom, my boyfriend's dead."

"Your what?"

Okay, so it's out there now, and Fox is kinda regretting it. "You heard," he says, but meekly, in a voice that's barely there. His idea about the printed cards and black crayon would have been so much easier, but he wasn't planning to do this.

"Your boyfriend?"

They've caught a red, so he can feel her looking at him. "I dunno." *Maybe Pete's right, maybe I am just trying to own him... no, who cares if we never used the word. That's what we were, boyfriends. All I know is,* "I loved him."

She reaches across the console, grabs for his arm, but he pulls away. "I didn't know."

He refuses to look, so she pets his hair.

"You two were so close. Honestly, sometimes I might have thought there could have been something, but I didn't know for sure. You could have told me, if you wanted. It doesn't make any difference to me. I hope you know that."

"What would Dad think?" He tries not to, but he cries.

Takes her a second to think that through... "Your dad would have thought it was so cool that you found someone you could care so much about."

Strange that something he's needed so badly to hear could enkindle such a terrible ache, but the message only amplifies his sense of loss, only makes him cry harder. If only he had his dad to comfort him now, the way he had Ethan when...

"He thought the world of your friends, Ethan and Pete both, and he was never anything, *anything* but proud of you."

"How could he be proud of me?"

"He was. So, *so* proud. Just like I am. Of all your talent. Your sense of humor. Your bravery."

"But it's my fault he's dead." *And now I've fucked up Pete's future, too.*

"How can you think that?"

"It's true."

"It's not."

"How do you know?"

"What he did was his choice. You know that, don't you?"

"Yeah," *but so what if it was? That doesn't absolve me.*

Her fingers find the split in his scalp, and he hisses.

"You're bleeding."

"I'm okay." He presses his forehead to the cool glass.

She parts his hair so she can examine the scabby damage.

He draws air through clenched teeth.

"Doesn't look too bad, but we need to put some antiseptic on it when we get home."

The car behind them honks. The light's turned green. She withdraws her touch and drives on.

The fluctuations in speed knock Fox's head against the window, sending sharp pain radiating through the swelling knots, but he doesn't pull away because there's something soothing about the cold, something he needs from it. "I miss him so much."

"I know you do... maybe we ought to think about getting you some help."

"What help?"

"Someone to talk to."

"I don't need any help. I just need him back."

"Am I gonna be grounded?" Fox asks as she sees him to bed.

"Maybe. I dunno. You get some rest, and I'll think about it."

Yeah, but up here the skulls are taunting him. Especially the motion activated ones with chattering teeth and light-up eyeballs that go off mocking him, every move he makes, his own canned audience to punctuate the sick joke that is his tragic life. *What's so fucking funny about it?*

He coughs up more of the death dust that's invaded his sinuses, stirred up by all the crying. He holds the vile phlegm in his mouth until he can get to his bathroom and spit it into the sink, send it down the drain with a gush of water.

When he returns to his room, he's treated to another round of crowing ridicule. He takes his thermos from his backpack, chugs what's left of his suicide.

He plucks his horned Ethan mask from the wall, takes it to the mirror, and superimposes the ghostly expressionless countenance over his own. Reduced to colorless forms, there's a resemblance. He steps closer, presses his face right up to the glass and cocks his head, copping the demeanor of a masked horror villain. He stares through the eye holes at his reflected pupils, twin abysses, black holes, sucking him in.

He loses himself there.

It's the sound of distant thunder that finally breaks the spell and brings him home. He peels Ethan's stone visage from his own, tosses it onto the bed.

He changes into his windbreaker and damp boardshorts, loads his keys, cash, phone into his side pocket, then out the window he goes, down the side of the house and into the rain.

ELEVEN

FOLLOW THE LEADER

Raindrops crackle against the repellant fabric of Fox's nylon jacket as he shuffles upstream, kicking through the gush of water that races along the curb. This'll be the fourth time he's walked by Ethan's house. He keeps circling, thinking maybe next time he'll find the nerve to go to the door. Ethan's dad's car is in the drive, so Fox knows he's at home instead of work, where he otherwise would be if the world wasn't just so totally fucked. Maybe that's what's putting him off, the fear of facing the only person in the world who might be more destroyed by all this than he.

He sweeps the drippy blades of hair off his face as he comes upon the house once more. He's promised himself he's gonna do it this time, ring the bell and expose his guts to whoever answers, even if that turns out to be Mr. Enders. He doesn't know yet if he'll stick to his relationship with Ethan or cop to the cave as well, but he kinda thinks once he gets going he'll probably turn himself fully inside out, take them there and let them see for themselves how he's to blame.

He convinces his feet to stop, so that's progress. He stands at the edge of the yard puffing breath clouds. How many times has he walked straight up that lawn or gone around the side and climbed the fence to Ethan's window without so much as a second thought? He'd rather go anywhere else now, anywhere else in the world. Not that there's anywhere he actually wants to be. Not that he wants to be at all. Least of all, here.

I'm not nearly drunk enough for this, he tells himself, and considers heading home to raid his dad's liquor cabinet. But Mom would probably catch him, march him straight back up to the ossuary, only this time he'd be grounded for sure. No maybe about it. He can't risk it. This is something he has to do today. But first, a boost.

Five people have come and gone in the fifteen minutes Fox has loitered under the awning outside the corner store, tucked from view of the clerk between two ice machines. Of those five, he's approached only two, and neither reacted too favorably to the scruffy, bruised teen waving a ten dollar bill, begging a little help. One, he downright startled, so preoccupied she had been with getting out of the rain that she didn't even see him until he was practically on top of her.

So, yeah, no luck so far, but here comes another shot. A beat-to-hell old Toyota Camry splashes into a front parking spot. Metallica, Megadeth, Meshuggah stickers. Soulless growling bullshit blasting. Good signs. Couple of metalheads step out. Big guys, big arms, bulging guts. Goatees, camo, wallet chains. *Allies*, Fox thinks.

He moves in, delivers his pitch.

The bigger of the two snatches the ten. "Whatchu want?"

"Mad Dog, blue raspberry."

"Whatchu do, I just kept this?"

"I'd kick your ass," Fox says and means it, but that doesn't stop the guys going off like a couple of hyenas. Between the two of 'em, they've easily got three fifty, maybe four hundred pounds on him.

The biggun wads the bill and throws it at Fox, bounces it off his forehead. "Why don't you go see if Mommy has a juice box for you."

"Yeah, go play Nintendo, you brat."

"Go share a wooden dildo, you fucks."

"Ouch, splinters," Big Boy says, picking a wedgie as they enter the store, cackling.

Fox reclaims his wadded bill from an iridescent puddle, shoves it in his jacket pocket. He watches through the windows as the goons load up on snacks and beer. *Fuck this*, he decides, and goes in.

He buys time checking out the sunglasses, spots the clerk reflected in the carousel mirrors, eyeing him suspiciously, so he moves to the magazines, lingers until the metalheads take their shit to the counter, begin checking out. That's when Fox makes his move. His route takes him down the candy aisle, to the wall of freezers, where he spots the beaded vanilla mandarin drinks they used to come in for all last summer. He briefly considers abandoning the plan and just buying a couple of bottles. One for him, one for Pete. Decent peace offering.

No, that ship has sailed.

The goons ask for cigarettes, so the clerk turns his back on the store. No better time than now. Fox snags a bottle of

Mad Dog, stuffs it in his waistband and makes for the door.

"Hey!" Big Boy shouts, gruff enough to stop Fox in his tracks. "What you got under your jacket?"

"Nothing."

"Kid's ripping you off, man."

"Lift your jacket," the clerk says.

Fox does, and they see, so the clerk waves him over. Fox takes the bottle from his waistband.

"Busted." Big Boy giggles, scratches at his Metallica shirt.

"Hey, guess what..." Fox reaches into his jacket pocket, wads his soggy ten. "Metallica sucks, asshole."

"What did you say, you little shit?"

Fox pitches the balled bill and blasts out into the rain. The thugs tear off after him, but even with his shit knee, Fox is a hundred times faster. He glances over his shoulder as—

Big Boy trips up on uneven pavement and sprawls, skids across the wet asphalt on his belly, as if riding a great big slip-n'-slide. His friend busts up laughing.

Fox scales a fence and makes off across someone's backyard.

Hypnotic, the way the surge folds upon itself. Maybe it's just because Ethan so loved the rain, but Fox likes the creek this way, pumping with fevered enthusiasm, sky-tears pattering through the canopy.

The chase got him coughing, spitting up coal-stained phlegm as he winds through the trees, following the flow to sanctuary...

But upon arrival, he finds the cave entry every bit as

repellant as Ethan's house, finds insurmountable resistance to the prospect of submersing himself into the malaise, of taking more death dust into his overburdened system.

He slumps to a seat on the opposite bank, breaks open the bottle.

He keeps thinking he should practice what he's gonna say when they open the door. But each time he sets the scene in his mind, it's Ethan's dad who answers and it gets so intense, Fox just totally blanks, spaces out for minutes on end.

His side pouch lights up, vibrates. He draws his phone, overhangs it to shield from the rain. It's Mom calling, so she's realized he left. He rejects the call, pockets the device, turns up the Mad Dog, chugs a quarter... third... half the bottle.

He can't put it off forever. He made a promise to Ethan.

Go now. Just get it over with.

He rises, and *whoa*, okay, realizes he's far drunker than he thought. He stumbles, catches himself on a tree, then shuffles into the turbulent stream, staggers across and throws the saplings aside, then drops into the shallow dig. "Hold my blue razzbry," he slurs and tucks the bottle among Ethan's morphing blooms. He cups his hand to his mouth, whispers down the Sphincter, "I'm gon' go tell him now, k?"

Fox sways drunkenly at the edge of Ethan's yard, rain pouring over him.

Don't be a pussy. Just do it.

Yeah, *whatever*. Here we go...

He marches across the lawn, punches the doorbell, and

waits, wrestles with a powerful urge to ditch, like he and Pete used to do to random houses on their nightly summer prowls. They may even have hit this one before they knew who lived here. In fact, he's almost sure of it. The deadbolt rattles, clicks, so that option's struck.

Guess who answers the door? And he looks worse than Fox could possibly have imagined. Unshaven, hair cowlicked to hell, T-shirt neck stretched and sagging, as if he hasn't changed in days. But the thing that really scares Fox is the way his face looks. Nothing physical, nothing to do with the bags under his eyes, or the gauntness of his cheeks, although they certainly contribute to the effect, but some ineffable quality in the expression, or maybe missing from the expression, like most of him's lost, or dead. What's left cocks its head a degree or two, showing vacant wonder. The guy's had a stroke or something.

It was a mistake to come here.

Fox backs off the porch and into the rain, tortures the front of his jacket with both hands. *I'm sorry, I'm sorry*, his countenance pleads well before he manages to gape his jaw and vocalize the same.

Ellie joins her dad at the door. "Fox?"

"I tried to help him, I tried my best, but it was too late. I was too late."

"I know, we know that," she says.

"I don't know what to do."

Ellie clenches her eyes. "There's nothing we can do." She's clearly struggled to come to that herself.

"What's going on?" Ethan's Mom, Gina, asks, and joins her family on the porch.

Instinct carries Fox a further step toward the street.

He's drunk, Ellie mouths.

"Come inside," Gina says. "Fox, please."

"I didn't mean to let him go."

"We know."

Graham steps out from under the cover of the porch, into the rain.

Fox counters his advance with a retreat of the same distance. "I just needed you to know..." He says, lip quivering.

Do it. Tell them. Goddamnit, tell him...

"I love him. I love him so much."

Graham makes his move, Captures Fox's arm and spools him into a hug. "I know."

Fox always loved the smell of this house. That hasn't changed, but the scent's overwhelmed by the noxious fumes put off by all the flowers. Ellie runs to grab towels, Gina to start a pot of hot chocolate, so Fox and Graham drip together in the foyer, studying reflections of their own transformations in each other.

"Here ya go," Ellie says, and offers a sympathetic smile along with a towel.

Feels so fucking wrong to be here, accepting their hospitality and their pity. If they only knew what he said that night. If he'd only kept his fucking mouth shut, maybe they'd still have their son, brother. Ethan would be upstairs now, where he belongs.

"Come with me," Graham says and leads the way.

Fox follows uneasily, Ellie watching from the foot of the stairs as they depart, an expedition party of two, venturing into hostile territory. That's the impression Fox gets, anyway.

The ascension takes them into a chillier climate. The closer they get to the top of the stairs, the dizzier and tinglier Fox gets. Reaching the summit, he glances back down the covered ground, scans for Ellie, but she's vanished.

Fox's phone buzzes. Mom again. He doesn't even have to look. He lifts his leg and silences her through his shorts.

They pause outside Ethan's bedroom door. Fox swallows hard, closes his eyes and plummets backwards into his dilating skull cavern, into his own mental hellscape, which replays for him his endless torment—

What do you need me for?

Good question.

When he peels his eyes, Graham has gone in. Fox follows, finds him perched on the edge of the bed, digging through Ethan's backpack.

"I keep coming in here. I dunno what I think I'm gonna find. I guess I just need to know if there was something I missed, some reason why."

So they're more alike than Fox even guessed. While he's been exploring facsimiles of Ethan's bedroom in the cave, Graham's been scouring the real thing, driven by the same desperate need to answer an unanswerable question.

Graham withdraws a notebook, flips through the pages. "Found something in here the other day I thought you should see."

Fox can't decide if he's supposed to sit or not, but he doesn't want to be presumptuous, so he clings to the nearest bedpost, scratches his left calf's itchy abrasions with his right toes.

"I didn't make the connection at first, but—" Graham looks up, as if waiting for Fox to join. "Here."

Fox settles next to him. Graham hands him the

notebook, points out one of the many doodles in the margin. A fox, crudely drawn, but a fox nonetheless, bushy tail and all.

"That's just one. There's more throughout."

Fox flips forward, finds another... and another... running, jumping, sleeping, playing. Lots and lots of little foxes. So many that the simple, crude sketches can't help improving deeper into the book.

Fox's insides go looney. He feels about a hundred different ways about it.

"He really thought the world of you."

Fox bleeds the ink with a fallen teardrop.

"I dunno how I missed it, the two of you."

Fox senses Graham's gaze, hot as an intensely focused spotlight beam, sweeping all over his surface. Fox thinks of giving the man his eyes, letting him see inside. But if he did, he'd lose it. So he keeps his nose pointed into the book until he feels the relief of Graham's withdrawing scrutiny.

"I keep thinking there must have been so much else about him I missed... I just don't know why he couldn't talk to me."

"It's not your fault." *It can't be; it's mine.*

Graham acknowledges the sentiment with a forced smile. "I thought we were through the darkness, I really did. He seemed so much happier, these last couple years. If I'd known he was still hurting, I would have found him another doctor, pushed to try a different prescription. I would have done anything. That was my job."

"I didn't know he was depressed." Not clinically, anyway. Fox always sensed a sadness in Ethan, but that's just the way it is, isn't it, with really smart kids?

"For a long time now."

"He told me once about the time you took him to Pride. I think that was maybe his favorite memory."

Graham's eyes jam shut, face twitches. He fights a losing battle against his own tears.

"He wanted to tell you about us," Fox breaks, "but I wouldn't let him."

"Why?"

"I dunno, I dunno why."

"Well," Graham says after some time, "I'm glad he had you."

"I need him." *I wish he knew that. I never meant to make him think I didn't.*

"I do too."

"I told him I didn't." Fox doesn't dare look, but he feels Graham transforming in his periphery.

"What?"

"That night. I didn't mean it. It was only a joke. He said 'what do you need me for,' and I said 'good question,' and I don't know why, I don't know why I said that. I just know it's my fault. It's all my fault."

Graham draws Ethan's backpack to his chest, hugs it tightly.

"I'm so sorry." Fox stands. "I just needed you to know, I love him."

"Fox, wait."

But he doesn't. He takes off tromping down the stairs.

Gina intercepts him in the foyer as he fights against disequilibrium, fights to cram his feet into his sopping shoes. "You don't want any hot chocolate?"

"No, but thank you, though." He falls against the wall.

"Come, sit down."

"I'm okay, I'm okay."

"It's pouring. Let me call your mom."

A phantasmal silhouette stands at the top of the stairs. It's voice practically booms. "I'll drive you."

"I like the rain," Fox says and runs out into it.

The sun's pretty well expired by now, and the void's sucking at the warmth it left behind, nibbling at Fox's nose and ears as he trudges through the foamy rising creek water, hauling his exhausted, shivering body back to Ethan, or what remains of him, leaving a trail of breath clouds hovering in the rain-streaked atmosphere.

Upstream, the water climbs the beach of the boys' refuge, advancing towards the mouth of the cave, threatening to drown it if things don't let up, and soon.

Fox drops into the flooding dig. "He knows now. I told him," he says, teeth chattering as he strokes the blooms. "It was pretty much the worst thing ever, but I told him." He dredges the bottom, finds his submerged bottle and brings it up. Moonlight waltzes all along the shiny wet edges.

Pretty.

The cap disappears into the soup and a mouthful of blue poison disappears into Fox's gut. "An' I told him too how it's my fault, so he wouldn't have to think it's his. So don't worry about that, if you were."

The waterfall rages, bolstered by the inflow, threatens to wash Fox over the edge as he backs his drunken ass over the drop and negotiates his one-handed descent down the two-way bluff, bottle clanking violently against the folding and unfolding convolutions of the crag, against its flowering totems.

Mr. Fishy surfaces below, circles the tempestuous waters in anticipation of a yummy meal.

"I'm not gonna fall, stupid."

He finds a toehold in a blossoming pocket that resolves into Trent Reznor's crooning mouth. "I wanna fungh—"

The jaw snaps, sends Fox skidding down the angled escarpment, raking wildly for a catch, which he finds in a tangle of slithering bass guitar strings. His hooked fingers pluck F, C#, D before he finds purchase.

Below, the ravening shark whips its tail.

"Why don't you nibble Ellie's legs if you're so hungry? Plenty'a meat right there, you dumb fish."

He leaps from too high, lands hard atop the blue-furred rock shelf and buckles, hammering his chin against his knees, pinching his tongue between his teeth, exploding the bottle in his hand.

He cries out in agony, picks at a big ass shard stuck in the lacerated heel of his hand. Blood pours thick and clotted, quickly overflows his cupped palm, but the glass is too deeply imbedded to remove.

"Hey, you! Come here, you shit!" Fox climbs to his feet, toes the edge of the lagoon, and slings his chum out into the choppy brine. "Come 'n get you sippy sip."

Mr. Fishy roars to the surface, startlingly near, and thrashes, positively goddamn berserk, whipping waves up onto the ledge.

Fox fumbles his retreat, whacks the wall. "That's all! S'all you get!"

He sees that his spatter has drawn the tiny skulls from

between the star boulders. They swarm to feast on the coagulated droplets.

Fox flattens himself against the wax flowstone and sets off sidestepping his way across the narrow ledge, blood dribbling over his shoes, the shelf, the roiled waters.

He reaches the spot where the mantle has crumbled to no more than an outcropping inch.

He feels himself tipping, recoils, bumps the wall and drops into a devouring swell that draws him deep into tangled loops of some soft, squishy rope. He fights to free himself from—

A snare of intestines, he realizes, wrestling with his own remains. Or those, rather, of his sacrificial doppelganger. He slips their clutch, only to face his very own decapitated face.

He spews a simmering scream and kicks for the surface, bobs like a buoy, spurting billowing red cumulonimbi. He grasps for the ledge, but a greater swell smashes him into the wall, then tows him far out from reach of it.

Flailing, he spots a highlighter-yellow dorsal fin slipping under. He plunges for a better look, but the storm has murked the waters, reduced visibility to a meter or two tops. Ay, there it be. Near as that. Sweeping mesmeric stripes across its electric flesh.

Fox paddles madly for the beach, surfing the forward cresting waves, and fighting like hell against their receding pull. His pawing hands scrape the sandy shallows. He prepares to touch down and wade in, but the tide withdraws. Safe harbor recedes before him. Glancing over his shoulder, he sees the razor maw surging forth to intercept. He yelps and dives, just barely eludes death as the sunglow-now-blood-red rocket drives him against the seafloor, drags him with its sandpaper-textured belly... then circles back out for another go.

I should just let it have me, Fox thinks briefly, then a powerful wave floats him, slams him against the shore, and then draws back to beach him. He pushes up onto hands and knees as his pursuer skids up behind, bringing the chase to dry land.

"Rawr!" it bellows, flipping and flopping, nipping at Fox's feet with its serrated chompers, flesh flashing spasmodically.

Fox hurls himself inland, far beyond biting range, and twists 'round to watch it flounder. "Go eat a dick, dumbshit," he says, giggling, and blasts both middle fingers as a crashing wave carries it out.

Safe now, he sees to his salt-stung lacerations. He bites his shoulder, yanks the shard, tosses it into the sand. He thumbs the bloody heel of his hand, flips back a flap of floppy skin that resembles a thin slice of cold-cut deli meat. He puckers the wound between thumb and middle finger, making it gasp like a fish. Okay, no. That makes him queasy, and the heat, the moreso. Blistering down here with the Cold Lights smashed to smithereens.

Fox sheds his jacket, careful to avoid contact with his palm. He wraps his hand in the tail of his damp T-shirt. He gropes his pocket for his phone, curious to see if he's missed any more calls from Mom. But the phone's dead, destroyed by its dousing. He hurls it away, then picks up his glass shard and heads off to his favorite cave chamber.

The bog has dried up, cerulean clay cracked into a puzzle of plates. Fox's own double, dumped off the side of the bed, is likewise desiccated, cemented into the droughtland, its husk now an arid biome; the cavity of its burst belly, den to rubber snakes; its hollowed head, hive and feast alike to a colony of tiny skulls, swarming by the thousands. Only the churning cobalt cauldron at the center of the room remains molten, albeit sludgier, its bursting bubbles belching petrichor.

Fox climbs astride Ethan, the long strands of his wild hair dripping between them.

"Is this okay?" Ethan asks, once lustrous eyes now dull as burnished steel, flesh bruised by a pyrite patina.

Fox shuts his eyes. He can't go on trying to rewrite the memory. He can say *yes* 'til he's blue in the face, but it won't change a goddamn thing. Instead, he simply wraps his arms around the cooling body, rests his head on its shoulder, and spaces out to the lulling rhythm of its rising and falling chest, synchronizes his own breaths to match.

"Does it hurt?" Summer asks. She's sitting with Pete on his bed, under his rain-pattered skylight, studying his raw face.

"Not too bad."

"Did you get in trouble?"

"Suspended."

"What about finals?"

"Dunno yet."

"What were you supposed to do, just watch?"

"Guess, yeah."

"Are your parents pissed?"

"My mom's not. She likes Fox. My dad, I dunno, he doesn't know yet."

"S'good, at least, your mom's not mad."

"Yeah." Pete draws a sharp breath, tender to Summer's touch.

"Want me to kiss it better?"

He gulps. "Okay."

She takes his head into her gentle hands and presses her glossy lips to his, plants a prolonged peck. "Better?"

"May need something stronger."

"Oh," she says, laughing. "Well, try this, then." She presses their lips together once more, only this time, open.

Thusly cued, Pete's mom barges in.

Pete squeals, fumbles from Summer. "¡Ma! ¿Qué?"

She doesn't indulge his tantrum. "¿Sabes dónde está Fox?"

Pete notices she's muting her phone on her thigh. She need not explain further. He leaps from bed, snags his cell. His thumbs tap a frantic rhythm: *hey / where you at / I know you're pissed, just please respond so I know you're okay.*

His heart pounds ferociously, awaiting a response that never comes.

Something's really wrong.

"¿Nada?" his mom asks.

"No sé. No está respondiendo," he says, playing it cool, although he's flooding with adrenaline and beginning to tremble.

She switches to English, presumably in anticipation of jumping back on with Fox's mom. "Let me know when you hear?"

"Yeah, of course."

"And leave this door open..." She trails off, phone to ear.

"Fox is missing?"

Visions of Pete's dreams return to him. Premonitions,

maybe. He wedges his bare feet into his loosely-tied sneakers.

"Where you going?" Summer finds her own shoes.

"He's at the creek."

"How do you know?"

"Wait here, okay?" If it's already happened, he doesn't want her to see. He kisses her head and blasts off, bounds the stairs in a single leap, and launches out the front door, into the freezing rain.

He jams his phone to his ear, hoping a call might succeed where his texts have failed, but he's routed straight to voicemail. "Shit!" He picks up into a jog, into a full-on sprint.

Fox presses his lips to Ethan's ear, whispers, playfully spooky, "I'm coming to find you, Ethan."

The proclamation stirs the thing to tears of mercury.

Undeterred, Fox backs himself into the corner, presses the glass splinter to the slit already started for him.

The ceiling fan blades wither and blacken, hang slack like the wilting petals of a great flower. The phosphorescent clouds contained within the dome (usually a warm shade of heat-lamp orange) swirl into a cold blue tempest. The posters tacked across the craggy walls molder and peel, fall to the cracked clay in shriveling tatters. The central bog ceases belching petrichor and instead produces a perfume of copper—of *blood*—verging on rot.

What about Pete?

Doesn't need me, has Summer.

And Mom?

Don't think about her. She'll be okay.

Yeah, *okay.* So, here we go...

He barely begins to apply pressure, and yet the pain seems already insurmountable. The alcohol's done nothing to numb things.

"Fuck! How did you do this?"

Don't look at it. Don't think about it. Just draw a little line. Easy, when you think of it that way.

Pete wades carefully up the inflowing storm waters to the edge of the intensified waterfall and cranes his neck out over the drop, sees how unsettled the lagoon's become, sees it's spilled its banks, swallowed pool-skimmer Graham to the knees, sand-castle Ethan and Ellie to their chests. The merest sliver of beach remains. Its fingers of lava boil the waves, shroud all in great firelit palls of steam. Within minutes, that patch too will be devoured, and exit will require a swim through shark infested waters.

Pete yells Fox's name. The only response: his own voice returning to him in a flutter of reverberating whispers that wet his ear canals, tingle his scalp. He suppresses his terror, backs over the edge, and scales his way down the morphing wall.

The frenzy-fleshed hammerhead thrashes in the choppy waters, mad with bloodlust as Pete drops onto the outcrop, soles crunching broken glass.

And blood.

Everywhere dribbled, coagulating, tiny skulls gorging.

Pete calls again for Fox, certain now the deed is done. More certain still when only silence returns.

He mounts the ledge, works his way across, waves nipping at his ankles, threatening to draw him in. He slows to take the narrow stretch, and a cresting swell lassoes his legs with guts and entrails. Pete cries out for his friend before he spots its head and realizes; that ain't his Fox, too young. He steps out of the knot and hastens on, leaps ashore.

"Fox!" Pete yells, again.

It can't be too late. *Can't be.*

Suddenly, the little boy in the shallows—that tiny Ethan—turns his head towards the locker room, lifts his arm from the waves, and points.

What choice does Pete have but to trust him?

He blasts into the tin labyrinth, finds the gym-clothed teenagers already pointing the way. He follows, into the showers. The wet tiles glint with an intense flashing light thrown out from Ethan's bedroom ahead. He shudders, entering atmosphere so charged, he can almost feel tiny electrical arcs sizzling between his bristling neck hairs. Nearer the threshold, his nostrils flare at the scent of blood.

He prepares himself for the worst as he enters the desiccated bog, shielding his eyes from the glare of the spasmodic pulsar.

There he is, atop the bed, next to Ethan, sawing non committedly at his lacerated wrist.

Pete draws a whistling gasp, draws, at that, Fox's gaze.

"I dunno how he did it."

"Stop!"

Fox coughs. Black spittle spatters his chin. "I just want this to be over."

"No, you don't."

"It feels like hell."

"It's this fucking place. It gets inside you."

"It's all hell. There's nowhere I can go."

"I know it feels that way, Fox, but please. You're just drunk now, so this seems like a really good idea. I promise you it's not. So just give me that, okay, please." Pete puts his hand out, his desperation intensifying by the second.

"I didn't get a fair chance. Why couldn't I have had a fair chance to help him?"

"I don't know."

"I needed you."

He doesn't just mean this past week, Pete understands. He means after his dad, too. "I'm here now, okay? I'll stay with you, whatever you want. We'll explore every inch of this place together, if it makes things better for you, I promise. Just you and me, whatever you need. But you have to come with me now, okay? The cave's flooding. We can come back, but right now we have to go, so just drop the glass and come on."

"I can't live with this..." It sounds like there's more, but tears choke him up.

"This what?"

"This guilt." Fox shuts his weary eyes, as if for respite.

"Let it go."

"I can't."

"You have to. He did this to his goddamn fucking self, Fox. He did this to *you. Fuck him!*"

"Don't you fucking say that."

"Are you really gonna do this to your mom? Leave her all alone? Make her feel how you feel right now? How fucking selfish are you?"

Fox turns his attention back to his forearm, applies pressure, as if in spite, making blood gurgle.

The tempestuous swirling stardust goes supernova, liquifies the ceiling fan dome in a flash of blinding phosphorescence before blinking out, leaving the room in a darkness absolute but for the pale glow put off by a spatter of turquoise lava that falls over the churning indigo bog, inciting a hissing eruption of noxious steam.

Pete pounces, gropes for the shard.

Fox screams, ferocious. "Get off me!"

Pete pries the glass from his grip.

"Give it back!"

Pete runs out to the grotto, hurls the blade into the lagoon, and turns back just as Fox rockets him into the surf.

Pete rights himself—"Fuckin' hell, Fox?"—only to be tackled again.

The boys wrestle as a wave smears them across the submerged shore, and very nearly, a finger of lava.

"Stop!" Pete shouts between breaths, But Fox is relentless. "Fucking asshole, *stop!*" Pete manages to extricate himself just as a giant swell breaks over them, sending a cascade of foamy white brine crashing against the far wall. The resulting undertow drags Pete from Fox, pulls him out to where his feet barely touch.

"Pete!" Fox screeches, suddenly goddamn hysterical—

And then Pete's ripped underwater, into a cloud of his own blood.

Fox's hands shoot to his head as he momentarily digests the horror. *Oh shit, oh fuck. What have I done?* Then, without any regard for his own safety, he dives.

He finds them through the murk and bubbles and red cirrus streaks, Pete fighting futilely against the hypnotically flashing beast that's claimed his thigh. The boys share eye contact, pure terror, as Fox joins the melee, concentrating his efforts first on prying the jaws, then failing that, full-on animal assault. He sinks his incisors into a strobing fin, claws the animated flesh, catches the gills, and laces his fingers into them.

Its nictitating eye flicks to its assailant.

You can't fucking have him.

Fox rends a great big strip of electric flesh.

That wins Pete's release. The injured shark jets away.

Pete flails desperately for the surface, no easy task with his lame leg. Fox hooks him under the armpits and brings him up, gasping.

"Is my leg there? Is my leg still there?"

Fox swims Pete to the blue-furred outcrop by the waterfall.

Pete gropes for the edge, but the surface plunges; they tread the trough until another swell boosts them. "I can't believe you fucking did this."

"Go!"

Pete scurries for all he's worth, then spins around and throws out his hands.

But the tide drags Fox out of reach.

Over his shoulder, he glimpses the knife-like, stripe-swept fin cutting the waves, fountaining sea spray as it torpedoes him.

This is it, he thinks, and prepares himself to join Ethan, then a particularly large swell heaves him to the lip, where he finds two outstretched hands begging his. He surrenders his life to Pete just as the gaping jaws breach the foamy surface and snap shut on a mouthful of nothing. Pete yanks him clear.

"I'm sorry, Pete, I didn't mean it. I swear I didn't mean it."

Pete checks his damage. Blood pulses through his shredded jeans in thick clotting globs. He falls back, white as a ghost. "Holy fuck, that's alotta blood."

"No, it isn't," Fox says, but his bulging eyes and generally horrified expression say otherwise. "Remember that time you fell on the side of the pool? That was a hundred times more blood. This is nothing."

"It doesn't feel like nothing."

Fox very carefully parts the ripped denim, inspects the wound. It's not nothing, that's for sure.

"Is it bad? Is it call-nine-one-one bad?"

"You have your phone?"

"Oh fuck, it is? It's nine-one-one bad?" Pete draws his phone, but it won't turn on. Not now that it's been submersed. "Go get my mom."

"Really?"

"No-no, don't, don't leave me down here."

Fox whips off his soaked shirt, wraps it around Pete's thigh, making him writhe and hiss.

"You don't have any idea what you're doing."

"Yes, I do." Fox loops the fabric into a knot. "I'm slowing the blood."

"Don't tie it so tight, they'll have to cut it off."

"I don't care."

"Not your shirt, my leg!"

"Wait, what?"

"That's what happens."

Fox loosens the knot. "Can you climb, you think?"

"No fucking way."

"What if I piggyback you? Could you hang on?"

"You can't piggyback me up the fucking wall."

"Watch me."

"Fuck you."

"Fuck you, asshole. It's not that steep. Let's fucking go." He kneels for the mounting.

Pete reluctantly drapes himself over Fox's spine, gets a stranglehold 'round the neck as Fox struggles to erect himself.

"Let up, dickhead, you're choking me."

"You can't even lift me, dumbass, how's this gonna work?" Pete slips off, catches himself on his good leg, keeps himself hobbling upright by clinging to Fox.

"Just jump. It's easier," Fox says and squats.

Pete leaps aboard. Fox catches him and winces, simultaneously feeling the load in his bum knee and Pete's goopy blood in his right hand. He moves his fingers from the wound.

"Okay?"

"Think I'm gonna faint."

"Serious?"

"I dunno."

"Well, I'm not gonna start climbing if you're gonna fall off."

"I'm okay, just go." Pete locks his legs so Fox can have his hands.

Fox starts up the wall, ignoring his throbbing knee and the severe stinging of his lacerated palm, wrist.

Pete has to hop his own way up the ladder, into the night. Fox follows, astonished to discover how high the creek's risen, how violent is the flow. Seldom have they seen it this way. Never outside of hurricane season.

Fox takes Pete back on board, slogs upstream against the gushing current, determined like hell to get him to the street, but just shy of the culvert, his knee gives, leg folds, and they tumble into the surge, Pete yowling, Fox hacking up more charcoal-stained phlegm.

"I can't look, is it still bleeding?"

"Yeah, but it's not that bad, really."

"Don't lie."

"I'm not."

"Pete!" That's Summer! Yelling from the top of the culvert. "What happened?"

"Get help!" Fox screams.

Off she shoots!

Pete's head lolls. "I'm gonna pass out now." And he does.

Fox cradles his neck so he doesn't drown. "Pete? Pete!"

His eyes are open, but he's ain't home. Is he passed out, or—

Fox wails into the rain. "Help! Somebody, help!"

The screaming snaps Pete to with a sudden befuddled start. "Did I just faint?"

"Dude. Oh my god. Your eyes were open, it was so fuckin' freaky."

"Oh fuck, oh shit." Pete looks around, panting, struggling to regain his bearings.

"You okay?"

"I'm not gonna die." Although phrased as a statement, it comes out sounding more like a question.

"No, I know."

"You promise?"

"You better fucking not."

They make eye contact, cold waters gushing 'round

them, distant thunder rumbling, light traffic swishing across a nearby road, husbands, wives, mothers, fathers returning home from a hard day's work. The world spins ever-faster, but this moment belongs to Fox and Pete.

Pete offers his pinky. "I promise if you do."

Fox hesitates...

A welcome interruption calls from above. "Y'all okay?" Fox recognizes the voice. It's Graham!

"Help!"

Graham skids down the graffitied concrete slope.

"It's his leg."

Graham pulls the bloody dressing aside so he can judge the severity of the wound.

"Can you help me get him up?"

Graham scoops Pete into his arms and lifts. Fox can't help thinking how small and vulnerable, how childlike his friend looks, draped across a father's arms.

They get him up to the street just as an SUV skids to a stop before them. "What happened," Pete's mom demands, intimidating as all hell, as she and Summer spill out of the vehicle.

"I fell," Pete says.

Graham helps him to the backseat. "Looks like he probably needs stitches."

Fox tunes the rest out, retreats inward, into an image of home. His electric blanket, his dad's couch, a plate of pizza rolls, HGTV, and Mom—the most beautiful, wonderful mom in the entire world—there beside him.

When he opens his eyes again, Pete's being driven away. Graham takes off his coat and cloaks Fox's bare torso, discovers the lacerated wrist.

"I—" Fox says, teeth chattering.

"I know."

"I'd do anything."

"You know, everyone keeps telling me, 'it's not your fault, it's not your fault.' They don't know. They can't. But *I* know." He takes Fox's head into his hands. "You hear me? *I know*. It's. Not. Your. Fault."

"How is it not?"

"Because you gave him love."

Fox's lip quivers. Fresh tears flow, but the rain erases them.

Graham pulls him into an embrace, holds him a good long while, holds him until, at once it seems, the storm lets up. "Better get you home." He urges Fox to his feet, gets them walking that direction.

Fox casts his gaze to the speckled void, where one star—no, a plane—scrapes the others. He wishes upon it anyway—

I wish... I wish for Ethan to find a way to be happy, wherever he goes.

In Fox's bathroom, his mom tends to his wounds and asks all kinds of questions he doesn't want to answer. Finally, he just starts sobbing. "I don't wanna die," he says over and over again.

"You won't. Not for a long, long time."

TWELVE

A NEW BEGINNING

Christmas came and went, but winter lingers. It's the first day of a new semester, and Fox is actually glad to be back at school, if only for a respite from his mom's warden-like watch. He broke down that night, confessed everything—his alcoholism, his survivor's guilt, even his aborted suicide attempt—everything but the cave. She emptied the liquor cabinet, got him an appointment with a therapist, and enrolled him in a group, to hell with his protests. His cough persists, but the phlegm he's hacking up these days is mostly clear of the black cave residue. He hasn't been back. Not in two weeks, not since. But he hasn't stopped thinking about it, every second, every day, trying to hold onto what he can while the details sift like sand through his fingers. He's gonna go back once more when he works up the nerve, say goodbye and bury the entrance, put Ethan to rest, safe from unwelcome intruders. Maybe pluck just one piece to remember by.

The bell dismisses fourth period. Fox packs up his books and heads to the cafeteria. If he sees Pete, it'll be the first time since that night. Pete wasn't on the bus this morning, and Fox hasn't called or texted—even though he got a new SIM card put in his old phone—for fear of finding out Pete's done being dragged down by him. If he is, who could blame him? Fox did make his mom call Pete's, however, just to make sure he was okay.

Fox claims his place at their deserted table, unpacks his lunch. He scans the lacrosse guys, hoping for a glimpse. It'd just be nice to see him. But he's not there, so Fox goes to work untangling his earbuds.

"Whuddup," a voice says. Pete's. He sets his tray on the table and passes himself from his crutches to his old seat.

Fox fights against the big dopey grin he can feel crawling across his face, fights against the welling of his eyes. "Can I see?"

Pete hikes up the leg of his gym shorts, shows off the damage. "Is that the most stitches you've ever seen in your life?"

"It's a shitload of stitches," Fox says, and laughs. "When do they come out?"

"Tomorrow, actually."

"What'd you tell 'em?"

"Said we were wrestling, 'n I fell on a broken bottle."

"They believed you?"

"Yeah, I guess."

"I guess it doesn't look that much like a bite. Does it hurt?"

"You have no idea. They gave me oxy. No, you can't have one."

Fox snorts, playing a good sport even if the joke hurts

him a little. "Kinda sucks you can't just tell everyone you got bit by a shark."

"Yeah, right?"

"Guess you won't be playing lacrosse for a while."

"Guess not, you dick. I'm kicked off the team anyway."

"Why?"

"Fighting."

"Sorry."

"Whatever, I suck anyway, 'n, you know, some things are more important."

Fox snorts, tickled by Pete's echoing of his sentiment. "I really am sorry."

"I know. You okay?"

"I have to go to therapy now."

"That's prob'ly good."

"I guess. I can't stand it."

"Why?"

"I dunno. Group's okay, I guess. There's this one dude, Nate, I sorta made friends with. He's a senior at Clements."

"Oh, a senior, do tell."

"Shut up."

Pete laughs. "You been back to the cave?"

"No, you?"

"Fuck no."

Fox cackles. "Your ladder's still down there."

"Leave it."

"I'm sorry, I haven't called."

"Yeah, me too." Pete hangs his head shamefully. It seems to weigh on him. "I dunno why I didn't."

"S'okay."

"I kept meaning to, s'just, I didn't have a phone, and then we were in Argentina for a week, and... you know."

Reading him, Fox senses there's something else too. An awkwardness there never was before. Not between them.

"You know, you never promised." Pete extends his pinky. "And I didn't die, so."

Fox stares at Pete's finger a moment, then hooks it with his own. "I promise," he says and means it.

"You better. The world would fucking suck without you."

"You don't have to worry about me. And you don't have to sit here, you know, just to be nice."

Pete scoffs.

"I don't mean it like that, I just mean if you'd rather sit with them, you should. I wouldn't blame you."

"I sit where I want, man. But Summer's gonna sit here too, and you better not be a dick."

"That's cool. Where is she?"

"Still in line." Pete points her out.

"What're you doing after school?"

"I'unno. You wanna go skate the Met?"

Fox laughs. "How are you gonna skate?"

Pete pantomimes pumping himself along on his crutches like a skier, gets Fox cracking up.

Then, silence.

Dreadfully sober, Fox asks, "Will you help me bury it?"

It's the sunniest it's been in a good long while, maybe only temporarily so, but Fox appreciates the warmth nonetheless. Pete inches his seated ass down the concrete slope of the culvert, meets Fox at the bottom and reclaims his crutches.

Before they head upstream, Pete pauses for a hit off his vape, offers Fox a puff.

"I'm good."

The creek's calmed to its usual slow gurgling pace. Matching Pete's hobbled gait along its banks, Fox can't help finding wonder in details he's taken for granted. The sparkles shimmering across the surface. The minnows skittering underneath. The crunch of dry leaves underfoot. The scent of a distant burning brush pile intermingling with the coffee aroma that wafts occasionally his way. The comfort of his present company. A world of beauty, if you want to see it.

Coming up on the refuge, his lifted spirits crash. He runs ahead, drops onto hands and knees—

The crater's already filled, the earth healed. "No-no!" He plunges both hands into the soil.

Pete hurries to catch up. "What are you doing?"

"I'm sorry, I'm sorry I didn't visit," Fox works feverishly to reopen the wound, but deep as he digs, he finds only dirt.

"Fox, stop."

"I just need a piece, just give me one piece to remember."

Pete goes down onto his knees next to his frenzied friend. Gentle yet commanding, he whispers, "Stop."

Fox checks Pete with an expression of utter desolation.

"We came here to close it."

"But I didn't get to say goodbye." A teardrop falls, waters the earth between his knees, precipitates the faintest wisp of petrichor.

The dirt rejects the tear, discharges it as a perfect hemispherical bead. Or, no. It's not the droplet the ground renders, nor fluid at all, but plastic. A tiny scuffed dome that shoves the soil as it swells rapidly to the size of an egg. A teaspoon of some red-brown ink seethes inside, congeals finally into a cockroach.

Fox lifts the capsule into his cupped palms and brightens with hope. Here again, the same strange fruit that first heralded the cave's arrival. He imagines taking it home, planting it in one of his mother's flower pots, watering it daily, and making sure it gets plenty of—but not too much—sunlight. He imagines how much of Ethan he might be able to regrow from it in time. He can see himself taking over his mother's flowerbeds, raising a garden unlike any other, ever vigilant to protect it from any black blight.

But as he watches the imprisoned insect's helpless scurrying, he's overwhelmed by an urge to set it free. So what if he loathes the things? So what if it represents the worst, the darkest parts of Ethan? The corruption of his most precious memories? It's a part of him nonetheless, and it deserves to be free. And so does Fox, from this undertow Ethan swept him into.

He pops the cap and dumps the creature out. It plots a confused zigzag before breaking for the trees.

Fox snaps the plastic cap onto the dome, inserts it back into the ground, and swipes a pile of soil over it.

Goodbye, my love.

A chilly wind blows through, scatters dry leaves. Cold's coming back again.

Pete rests a consoling hand on Fox's shoulder. Fox leans into it, slumps against him, and Pete encircles him with his arms.

Winter's only just begun. The worst is still to come, but afterwards, spring, and then the summer of Fox's sixteenth birthday, a summer of firsts, of new adventures to be surpassed only by those still ahead. Fox's mom has already promised to help him out with a car if he pays the insurance and gas, and if he promises to abstain from drinking (and don't think she won't be keeping watch), and Nate-from-therapy said he could probably get Fox a job at the skate shop in the mall where he works. Fox is supposed to go meet the manager later this week even though his birthday is still a little ways off, but he's looking forward now, and not just living impulse by impulse.

He gets why they worry, Pete and his mom, but Ethan made his choice, and Fox has made his. Maybe there is something romantic about a young life cut tragically short, but there's a greater romance to a young life yet unlived, with every possibility flourishing before it.

Already, his experiences below feel as if from a distant dream. Years down the road, Fox can see himself fully grown, with husband or wife, perhaps children of his own, reflecting occasionally on this time as the cold, rainy winter something so terrible happened that the very nature of reality itself was temporarily upset. He'll think back to the cave, remembering it only vaguely, as something beyond description, beyond language. He'll remember Ethan the same, with ever-diminishing detail, as a special friend who gave up everything before it even began.

For now, Fox closes his eyes and conjures him. That's where Ethan will live, an imprint blossoming anew upon each remembering, only fainter, ever fainter.

ACKNOWLEDGMENTS

My eternal gratitude to Anthony Mattero, Alex Rice, Jordan Berg, Jiah Shin, and Lee Stobby for championing my dreams, and to Mark Alan Miller for realizing this one.

www.ingramcontent.com/pod-product-compliance
Lightning Source LLC
Chambersburg PA
CBHW011036190726
48290CB00011B/2868